The Hunted

Back in Dodge, Clint Winslowe had, in self-defence, gunned down a couple of gunhawks who had bushwhacked him. Framed by a crooked sheriff, he had been brought to trial and sentenced to hang for murder.

Escaping from jail, he fled to the hills with lawmen of half-a-dozen states after him. But others were interested in Winslowe as well. The two men he had killed had been members of the notorious Carswell gang and their deaths had foiled one of the biggest stage robberies ever planned in the state.

With every hand turned against him, Winslowe must prove his innocence by finding the one witness who could have cleared his name at the trial. But why had she been willing for an innocent man to die?

By the same author

Justice at Red River

The Hunted

PHILIP ASTON

A Black Horse Western

ROBERT HALE · LONDON

ISBN 0 7090 7728 9

Robert Hale Limited
Clerkenwell House
Clerkenwell Green
London EC1R 0HT

Typeset by
Derek Doyle & Associates, Shaw Heath.
Printed and bound in Great Britain by
Antony Rowe Limited, Wiltshire

CHAPTER ONE

THE WILD ONES

Clint Winslowe had crossed the river three miles east of the town and made a noon camp in the shade of a small grove of trees that grew beside the sluggish water. Behind him lay fifty miles of waste, desert land where the heat was a burning pressure on a man's skull and a horse covered no more than ten miles in the day on a single bellyful of brackish water, where the dust devils rolled around the sun-punished ground and raised a half-seen turbulence on the burnt-brown desert, where a man's eyes would be blistered out of usefulness if he so much as lifted his head to stare at the glaring ball of the sun.

There had been few travellers on that trail. Men shunned the desert spaces and kept to the stage trail further to the north. But men who did not want to be seen by prying eyes suffered the burning hell of the desert country and came upon the town from the east. He chewed reflectively on the pieces of dried meat, drank thirstily from the canteen, knowing that for the first time in two weeks he had water in plenty, could fill it to the brim whenever he wished. There had been moments on the trail, bad moments, when he had figured it would be impossible to make it to the river, when the horse had dropped in the terrible heat and his belly had grumbled at the lack of food. But he was here and by sundown he could be in Chandler City at the foot of the mountains which were now visible through the heat haze.

The sorrel drifted to graze in the sparse grass while he built a smoke and stretched himself out in the shade. There was a deep weariness in the long, lean body and a rider's looseness about his limbs which marked him for a trail-herder or a gunslick. His face had been burned a deep brown by long exposure to the hot sun and the piercing blue eyes had a searching quality about them which men found disquieting.

An hour, two hours and the sun began to edge its way around the clump of trees, touching him with a scorching finger. He rose slowly to his feet, eyes three-quarter lidded against the glare. Whistling to the sorrel, he swung himself easily into the saddle, turned to make a wide sweep of the river bend, to approach Chandler City from the southeast. The middle-down sun burned warmly on his back but seemed to have lost a little of the fierce noonday heat which had made riding a soul-destroying torture during the past few days.

He deliberately gave the sorrel its head, not forcing the pace. When a man rode far he soon learned to ride slow, to give his horse a chance to pick its own gait, for in the desert in that blistering heat, a man's horse was often the only thing which stood between him and death. Somewhere ahead of him, probably in Chandler City, but possibly even beyond, in the mountain ranges which lay to the west, were the men he was seeking, men he had hunted down from Abilene through Comanche country and now here. He didn't know how many of them there would be when he finally caught up with them; all he did know was that he intended to kill them, shoot them down in cold blood – and if the law decided after that, that he was a murderer, then it could also take its chance with him.

His shadow ran before him throughout the long afternoon and evening. By the time the sun had dropped down below the horizon and the world suddenly switched from one of flaming reds and oranges, into a twilit world of steel-blue and grey. He felt the coolness of the night breeze flow against his face as he rode towards the town, washing some of the heat from his body. He felt less tense now, but there was a strange excitement still riding him, as it had ridden him for almost as long as he could remember. Sitting straight and tall in the saddle, he rolled himself a smoke, touched his tongue to the paper, then thrust the cigarette between his lips and lit it with a sulphur match.

Perhaps here, he thought inwardly, he might find the end of the trail. But there had been so many times in the past when he had ridden into a new town and thought this way – and always he had been disappointed. Sure, they had told him, men answering the description he gave had been there, two, maybe three weeks before. But they'd ridden on and nobody knew where they'd gone.

The town sat on both sides of a long, winding creek, a single bridge spanning the smoothly running water. It faced the desert and the long, tall hills at the back as well and now that the sun had gone down, there was a coolness in the dusty street as he rode slowly in, eyeing the double row of scattered buildings on either side of him alertly. There had been too many attempts on his life in the past year for him ever to relax his vigil. Beyond the buildings, just visible in the encroaching darkness, he could see where the road lead straight out of town, heading due west until it reached a deep, steep-sided canyon and vanished from sight. There were lights in several of the low-roofed houses and in the middle of the town, where two roads met and crossed, more lights shone in the saloon windows and through the open doorway of a hotel which stood on one corner of the small square. Beyond the 'Trail's End' saloon, he noticed a stable and headed his horse towards it. The few people out on the streets barely gave the tall cowboy a second glance. From the corner of his eye, he saw one of the gaudily dressed women from the saloon eye him archly, boldness in her face, then she turned away as he rode past.

A man drifted out of the dark shadow of the stable, took the reins of the horse as he swung himself wearily out of the saddle, looked closely at him in the dimness. Clint had an impression of close-set, shifty eyes and a narrow face. Then the man said quietly: 'You figuring on staying here long, stranger?'

'Could be. Depends on whether I find the men I'm looking for.'

The other's brow went up into a hard, straight line. 'If you're looking for trouble, reckon you might find it around here,' he said thinly. 'Most every wanted man there is comes to Chandler City sometime.'

'Reckon you might be able to help me then.' Clint hitched the twin Colts higher around his waist and flexed his fingers a little.

'Mebbe.' The other led the sorrel away to one of the stalls, bedded it down for the night, then came back and stood close to him. 'You know why I work here, mister? Because I see everything that goes on in this town without getting into trouble myself. It's a bad town. No law here. Last sheriff lasted two months. Now he's buried up there on the hill along with five others.'

'Is there no sheriff here now?' asked Clint.

The groom shook his head. 'Nobody feels like taking the job. They reckon the Carswell Gang are somewhere around, up in the hills. Never seen 'em myself, but I'll take people's word for it.'

Clint offered him a smoke, waited while the other rolled it blind, then struck a match and leaned forward, studying the man's face in the brief flare. He saw the thin lips compressed into a tight line as the groom breathed deeply on the cigarette, saw the pale blue eyes that bored into his, knew that the other was just as curious about him.

8

'I see a lot and I know a lot,' went on the groom harshly. His eyes darted along the street as a group of men came out of one of the saloons and walked swiftly across the street into the boardwalk at the other side. 'You looking for any of the Carswell brothers?'

'What makes you think that?' parried Clint.

'No real reason. You've got the look about you. Either you're being hunted or you're doing the hunting, can't quite figure out which right now.' He made it into a hopeful question, teetering on one foot, a deep curiosity glittering in his eyes.

'Those hills out there stretch clear to Dodge,' said Clint quietly, musingly. 'If the Carswells are in there as you reckon, it'd take a while to smoke 'em out. You got any ideas where they might be hiding out?'

'Nope,' the other shook his head. The tip of his cigarette glowed redly in the dimness. 'But now and again, they're supposed to come down into town, have a poker game in the saloon yonder, pick up some supplies. But that ain't often and you'd stand a better chance of finding 'em in Dodge.'

Clint doubted that. If there was no law here in Chandler City, this was the logical place for the Carswells to come for supplies. Particularly as it seemed they were the reason for nobody wanting the job of sheriff. He decided to scout around the town for a while, check in the saloons and hotel. If there was any scent of them here at all, he'd know what to do. If not, then he'd take this man's advice and head west for Dodge.

A sudden yell from the heart of the town and a bunch of riders came into the street, the dust lifting from around the hoofs of their horses. Clint moved away into the boardwalk, edged along the front of the store, then paused for a moment near the hotel. The smell of food came appetisingly to his nostrils and the sharp pang of hunger pains in the pit of his stomach reminded him that he had been living on jerky meat for the past week while he had ridden over that sun-baked hell of the desert. A couple of men moved idly past him as he went inside the hotel, giving him a quick glance as he passed them. But there was no recognition on their faces and they were not the men he was looking for. Signing the register, he went quickly to the room up the creaking stairs. It was small, but well furnished and he swilled himself with the cool water in the pitcher before going back down into the small dining room. There was a deep thirst which had settled inside him over the long and dusty miles of grit and heat and it was going to take a lot to slake it, but he knew he had to get food inside him first.

While he waited for the meal to be brought in to him, he sat back in his chair, letting the tight muscles of his body relax, his gaze running over the faces of the few residents in the hotel. This was supper time, normally a slack time and there were fewer than a dozen people in the dining room. A couple of old ladies, primly-dressed in black lace, who stared down at their food all the time they ate, as if nobody else in the room existed for them. An obviously prosperous man in one corner whose quick, jerky gaze gave the impression that he was afraid of somebody, a man who did not enjoy his meal, who kept eyeing Clint closely from beneath lowered lids as if unable to make up his mind about him.

The others were the usual people one found in a frontier hotel such as this. The drifters who came in for an evening meal, a bed for the night before moving on again in the morning shortly after sun-up. Perhaps he could be classed as one of them, he reflected dryly. His meal came and he ate slowly, fully enjoying the laziness and luxury which followed so many hard days of riding in the glaring heat of the desert sun He felt dried up inside, brittle, as if the blazing sun had somehow sucked all of the moisture from his body, leaving it as stiff as a board. In front of him, his fingers kept flexing themselves automatically, as if they possessed a will all their own, knowing that whatever happened, someday he would

10

meet up with the men he had come out here, hunting, and then his hands would need all their old speed with a gun.

The weariness was still in him when he finished his meal, but he knew that he could not afford to sleep yet. Getting to his feet, he walked out of the hotel, across to the 'Trail's End' saloon. Pushing open the batwing doors, he stepped inside. It was the usual set-up. A bunch of two-bit gamblers were operating some of the tables. A handful of men stood against the bar, watching him covertly through the large crystal mirror at the back. They had him sized up, he reflected inwardly, could guess what he was and why he was there. This was one hell of a town, he decided. A man would live here only so long as he could outdraw the men who were looking for him.

Restlessness bubbled up inside him as he ordered a whiskey, gulped it down, then nodded to the bartender for another. One of the men sidled up to him, stood close for a long moment, staring straight ahead, but obviously interested in him. Finally, he murmured: 'Heard that you were looking for the Carswell brothers, stranger. That true?'

'Could be,' said Clint cautiously. 'News certainly gets around fast in this town.'

'Reckon it's best to know something about a fella as soon as he hits town,' countered the other. 'That way, it saves a heap of trouble.'

'You got any reason for asking?' Clint turned and eyed the other closely. The man was obviously a gunslinger with hard, glinting eyes and a deep scar down one side of his face.

'Jest thought I could help you out,' went on the other thinly. Suddenly, he laughed harshly, 'Don't git me wrong, stranger. I figured you might be mighty glad to hear where you could pick up the trail of those killers. I got no interest in the Carswell brothers, but if you got such little concern for yore life, I reckon I c'n help you along.'

'Is this just another speech like that I got from the

11

groom?' asked Clint.

'Don't be too proud of any reputation you got as a gunman,' said the other. 'They're fast, every last one of 'em. And they don't fight fair. They'll gun you down from cover the minute they pick you up on the trail. There's damned little originality in the way they work. If one don't shoot you in the back, another will.'

'So,' murmured Clint.

The other shrugged heavily. 'Just figured you might like to know what you're heading into, stranger. Means nothing to me if you git yourself shot. They passed through here a coupla days ago. Headed west to Dodge. Last I heard, they were operating there. If you cut out first thing in the morning, you could pick 'em up there.'

'Mebbe I'll take your advice,' said Clint softly. 'Thanks for the information anyway.' He felt the old, familiar tension rising swiftly inside him, the sudden tightening of every muscle in his body.

'You must hate these gunslingers to ride out here after 'em. Jest why are you doing this, pushing out yore neck like this? Those five gunhawks will gun you down the minute you ride through Dodge and you know it. Yet you still seem determined to ride out there. Why?'

'Any reason why I should tell you that?' demanded Clint harshly. He swung angry, suspicious eyes on the other. 'For all I know, you could be in cahoot's with those killers, ready to tip 'em off that I'm riding out to meet them tomorrow so they'll be ready and waitin' for me.'

The other shrugged. His face was still hard, like the cheek bones were fashioned of granite just beneath the surface of the skin. There were grey flecks in his eyes. Clint guessed that he was a dangerous man to tangle with yet he seemed unduly anxious to part with this information and be helpful.

For a moment, the other stood stock still. Then, slowly, he moved his right hand until it came into view and for the first time Clint realized that the gunman had been keeping it hidden from him deliberately. The fingers were all twisted out of shape and quite clearly it would be impossible for the other to make any play with a gun with that hand.

'That's no bullet wound,' said Clint narrowly. 'Who did it?'

'Chet Carswell.' Bitterness grew deep in the other man's voice. 'Three years ago now. He and two of his brothers had me holed up in the hills. Kept 'em at bay until I ran out of bullets, then I tried to make a run for it.' He gulped down the raw whiskey in his glass, studied the image of Clint's face for a moment, reflected in the crystal mirror. 'Weren't no use though. They shot my horse from under me, knocked me cold with a slug across the scalp. When I came round, they had me hog-tied across a saddle, took me further into the hills to some hide-out of theirs. That was where they did this. You ever see that bullhide whip that Chet carries?

'No – guess you're one of the lucky ones.' He held up the maimed, twisted right hand again, turned it sideways for a moment, studying it closely, lips twisted into a bitter sneer. 'That's what he used on me, stranger. Me – Bart Wingate who used to be one of the slickest gunfighters this side of the Mexican border – first across my back and then on my right hand. When he'd finished, he knew I'd never draw this hand again. I swore I'd kill him then, but I don't stand a chance. One of his killer brothers would get me before I even got within gunning distance of him. Could be, though, that's why I want to help you find 'em and gun 'em down.'

'You figger I might be the *hombre* to do your killing for you?'

The other's eyes narrowed on him in appraisal. 'I've been watching you, mister, ever since you rode into town from the desert trail.'

Clint felt a tightness rising in him, momentarily sharp and decisive, then he forced himself to relax. 'How do you know I came in off the desert trail?' he demanded harshly.

'A couple of my men followed you after you left the river back there.' The gunman's voice came easy without any trace of tightness. He was on guard, though, Clint sensed that, alert to his presence and still a little doubtful and suspicious about him.

'Nothing better to do with their time?' The shifty-eyed groom's words came back to him, unbidden: *This is one hell of a town – no law and order and everybody watching everybody else, ready for the first wrong move!*

'Well – you didn't think you could ride into Chandler City without notice, did you?'

'Why not?' muttered Clint aggressively.

The gunhawk said tersely: 'You must be green, stranger. Here we make it our business to know something about every man who comes and especially which trail brings him here. Even in this town, there ain't many men who come by that hell trail to the south, through the desert. It must have taken you the best part of ten days, ten days of torture by heat.' He spoke musingly, almost to himself. 'You must be wanted bad by somebody to come all that way through the desert, or mebbe you figgered you could get here without being spotted.'

'Could be,' Clint said tightly. He finished his drink. turned his back on the bar and let his gaze wander over the rest of the men in the saloon. 'If you're right about the Carswells being in Dodge you might live to see a couple of 'em die at least.' His voice was cold, his grey eyes like chips of ice.

The other nodded once, made as if to say something more, then stiffened abruptly at the sudden sound in the street outside. A man yelled something thinly, a cry that could have been a shout of warning or defiance. Almost immediately afterward, a gun spoke in the darkness and a bullet smashed a window of the saloon. Clint's right hand made a sudden drop for his belt, came up smoothly with the speed and fluid movement of a striking rattler, the heavy

14

Colt balanced perfectly in his palm, ready to spit lead as soon as a target showed itself. But the tables were already being thrust back as the bunch at the bar and in the saloon rushed for the street, no longer thinking of their poker and stud games. Only the two-bit gamblers in their black frock-coats were still seated in the saloon, acting as if nothing had happened, calmly picking up the rolls of bills on the tables. Clint guessed that none of these men had failed to join the rush for the door out of fear. Each man would carry a Derringer under his frock-coat and each would be a deadly shot with the weapon, but they intended to take no part in any cowhand feud. They were here with one purpose in mind, to make money, fairly or otherwise, and that was the only thing they would fight over.

Swiftly, Clint moved away from the bar as more shots sounded outside, but for a moment, the gunman by his side, held him back with his left hand. 'This is no fight of yours,' he said smoothly, urgently. 'That'll be the Donovan bunch hitting things up again. He owns one of the big cattle outfits between here and Dodge. Got some idea in his head that the boys here have been rustling some of his prime beef.'

'And have they?'

'Very likely, I'd say,' admitted the other. 'They're a wild bunch in Chandler City. Rustlers, killers, gunslingers, card-sharps, you name 'em and I reckon you'll find 'em all here.'

Clint hesitated for a moment, then shook off the other's restraining hand. 'Thanks again for the information about the Carswells,' he said shortly. He pushed open the swing doors and stepped outside into the street, pausing on the very edge of the walk, blinking rapidly until his eyes were accustomed to the darkness. There was the quick, lean sound of a rifle shot from the other side of the street and a slug fanned his cheek before ploughing into the upright between his body and the building.

Flattening himself swiftly against the front of the saloon, he jerked his head in the direction of the shot, caught a glimpse of the dark figure which showed for an instant in a patch of light from one of the windows. His first shot passed within an inch of the other's body as the man, warned by some kind of instinct, moved swiftly to one side. Before Clint could fire again, there came the thunder of hoofs on the dust of the street and a further bunch of men came riding swiftly around the corner of the street, rifles blazing. Clint let his gaze ride above the men, further along the street behind them, saw what he had begun to suspect. Whoever had tried to pull this trick on the part of the rancher and his men, the tables were about to be turned on them. The wild ones of Chandler City could turn a trick faster than any other bunch, he thought, with a faint touch of admiration. Out of the corner of his vision, he saw the two lines of men spill out of the shadows of the buildings further along the street, behind the riders. Their shots were scattered at first, possibly in their haste to open fire before the riding men got out of killing range, but several of their bullets struck home. Clint saw two men stumble from their saddles, pitch into the dust and lie still. Then the sudden rush of horses reached the place where he was standing and one wild-eyed, riderless horse came blundering along the rail of the boardwalk towards him. It lashed out savagely with its feet, almost pinning him to the wall.

Instinctively, he pulled his body away, half-fell as another board crashed under the weight of the plunging horse. Confusion grew as the two groups of men began to advance slowly on the riders, now caught in a trap of their own making. Clint could hear one loud, booming voice raised above the rest as the riders began to mill around aimlessly in front of him, firing at every man they could see on the street. Glancing up, slitting his eyes, he saw the tall, round-faced man seated on a gigantic, coalblack stallion, the man who led this bunch of unruly cowhands.

'Ride 'em down, men! Ride 'em down! Shoot your way through this goddamned town.'

16

Even as he yelled the words at the top of his voice, Clint noticed that his men were beginning to rally. The dust kicked up by the ploughing hoofs of the horses was beginning to screen the riders from sight. He loosed off a shot at a tall, thin-faced man who suddenly turned his horse and tried to ride directly at him, through the break in the rails where the riderless horse had hammered down the uprights. The rider gave a loud cry and reeled back in his saddle, almost losing his grip on the reins. His gun dropped from nerveless fingers as he wheeled, the horse lunging desperately.

The big man was still pointing and shouting, trying to give orders above the din of gunfire. The horses were breaking under the mêlée of noise, difficult to control now. Swiftly, lowering his head, Clint scuttled along the boardwalk until he reached the edge of the saloon where another street ran at right angles to the first. As he crouched there in the gloom, he was suddenly aware of eyes on him, watching him closely. Swinging his gaze, beyond the line of advancing men, their guns blazing, he saw the woman watching him from a balcony on the far side of the street. For a moment, he had the impression that there was a question in her gaze as it locked with his. Then he glanced away swiftly, leaving himself with only a vaguely disturbing memory of a pale face and dark eyes, half-seen in the shadows. When he looked back again a few moments later, she had gone, the balcony was empty and behind him, Donovan was rallying his men in a desperate effort to break through the men who had thrown a ring of guns about him. Seconds later, urging their mounts savagely, they burst through the men still in the street, scattering them on all sides, throwing shots over their shoulders as they rode out of town.

Thrusting the Colt back into its holster, Clint turned and made his way slowly back to the saloon, pausing outside. There were men lying in the street, many men, some from the town and others, men who had ridden in with Donovan.

He ran a hand over his chin. The old ways of violence were still very much alive in these frontier towns, he reflected bitterly, and remembered that this was the very reason that he was here, to kill men. For a long moment, he watched as men from the saloon and one of the stores opposite came into the street, examined the men lying there then lifted them and carried them into one of the long, low-roofed buildings. A town of lawlessness – without order. He wondered briefly why Dodge, which was reputed to have an iron-fisted marshal in command, did not take over this town which lay only a few miles distant. Possibly, he thought, the marshal in Dodge considered that so long as Chandler City existed in its present state of lawlessness, there would be less violence in Dodge.

When the street was cleared, he went back to the hotel, up to his room, pulled off the dusty, travel-stained clothing and stretched himself out on the bed, staring up at the ceiling of the room, trying to form things out in his mind. At least, if Bart Wingate was to be believed and had no hidden motive for giving him information, he would find the men he was seeking somewhere close to Dodge.

But there were other things on his mind that night, things which had not been there when he had first ridden into Chandler City. The memory of that woman, dark-eyed, who had watched him with sudden, awakening interest from the balcony, knowing he was there, guessing at what he was doing. Who was she? he wondered, and why the sudden interest in him? He tried to figure it out, then gave it up.

He felt oddly worried about the fact that men had watched him ride in from the desert trail. That was something he hadn't counted on; and it meant he would have to be a lot more careful in future. If Wingate's men would follow him like that, picking up his trail and riding after him without him knowing they were there, the same might be said for any of the Carswell gang. Maybe they didn't know

18

he was so close on their trail; maybe they did. But there could be trouble waiting for him in Dodge, or even before he got there, if he did not keep his wits about him.

Stretching himself full length on the low bed, he closed his eyes and was asleep within minutes, his weary body surrendering to the comfort of the first bed he had known in close on two months of hard riding.

He woke refreshed with the hot sun flooding the room with light. Outside, there was the sound of a single rider in the street. Swinging his legs to the floor, he went over to the solitary window and glanced out, keeping his body out of sight of anyone in the street below. The rider was just disappearing out of sight around the bend in the street, half-hidden in the cloud of dust thrown up by the horse. But he saw enough of him to recognize him instantly. It was the man who had spoken to him in the saloon bar the previous night, the man who called himself Bart Wingate and who wanted him to kill the Carswells for revenge. A man with a twisted hand who could no longer go after those men himself and carry his own revenge through to its fulfilment.

Spilling water into the basin, be shaved, splashed his face, then dried it thoroughly, briskly. Buckling on the gunbelt, he went down into the lobby of the hotel, handed his key in to the desk clerk, then went through into the dining room. The food was as good as it had been the night before and he ate his fill. Finishing, he went out into the street. Here, there were no signs now of the fighting which had taken place there the night before. The town was quiet in the morning sunlight and shadows were huge around the buildings on either side.

At the stable, he picked up his sorrel. There was a different groom there and although he searched the stalls with a keen-eyed gaze, he could see no sign of the man he had spoken to earlier. Riding out, he paused to give his horse a drink from the long stone trough, waiting until it had taken its fill before swinging up into the saddle again. The sun was warm on his back as he rode out of Chandler City and took the trail which forked left to Dodge. As he reached the edge of town, something in him made him turn and look back over his shoulder, back along the white, dusty length of the street. A hundred yards away, standing on the verandah of one of the houses, he saw the woman watching him again as she had the night before. Something stirred deep within him and he held himself in with an effort. No wonder had ever stirred him like that before, he told himself fiercely, and cursed himself for being such a fool. There was no reason for him ever to suppose that she was really interested in him. Possibly she was wondering what a stranger was doing in the town and why he had thrown in his lot with the wild bunch, the rustlers, against Donovan – when it had really been no part of his quarrel. Now he was riding out and he would probably never see her again. Because if he found the men he was seeking, either they would die or he would and whichever way things turned out, he didn't think he would be heading back this way again. Once he had done what he had set out to do, he would keep on riding west, to that promised land – California.

For the best part of an hour, he kept to the trail leading west. He saw no one, but there was still the memory of Wingate riding out before him strong in his mind and after a while, caution got the better of him and he turned the sorrel's head sharply, swung off the trail, and began to climb, keeping the trail in sight, but riding steadily higher as he climbed the ridge which ran along the side of the tall hill, where the timber grew thick and he could stay hidden, and yet watch the trail closely at the same time.

The sun was now high beyond the undulating crests of the mountains further to the east and the tall trunks of the pines with the first of the new foliage on them, grew high about him, filling the air with a sharp scent that touched the back of his nostrils with a pleasant tang. The almost solid mat of the branches met over his head, shutting out most of the sunlight, except where it filtered through the trunks as he kept to the outer fringe of trees. Here there would be shade for most of his journey, he reflected. Down there on the dusty trail, the midday heat would be a stifling pressure like that he had experienced in the desert. His horse made no sound on the spongy undergrowth where the pine needles lay thickly and there was a deep, underlying stillness here among the timber.

He let his horse find its own gait. In the beginning, when his father and two sisters had been shot down by the Carswell gang, more than two years before, there had been a bitter, overriding haste, urging him on, forcing his pace. But gradually, over the long months, the bitterness had moved deeper into his mind until now it was a gnawing, but stabilising, ache The impetuous desire to meet up with these men, to shoot them down in cold blood, was no longer as strong as it had been. He had had plenty of time to think things out. Now, he wanted those men to know the identity of the man who killed them, to know why he had trailed them across half a dozen states, nursing his vengeance, a burden which was still hard to bear. But it had made him tough, had given him the need to become so fast with a gun that he had earned himself a reputation as one of the fastest guns in the west. If his reputation had travelled ahead of him and reached the ears of the Carswell brothers, it might have put them on their guard, making things a little more difficult for him than otherwise might have been the case.

By noon, two more ridges lay behind him and he guessed he had covered half the distance to Dodge. Although there was a dry, dusty heat in the air, he had escaped most of it among the pines and he rested, still among the trees, but on a small rocky outcrop where he could see the trail immediately below him, some half a mile away, a narrow ribbon of white which stood out against the rest of the country. There was a cloud of dust lifting in the distance, in the direction of Dodge and he watched it with a quickening interest. It was too far away for him to tell if it was made by a band of hard-riding men or a stage, but as it drew closer, he saw that it was the stage, making its daily trip into Chandler City. Two men rode with it, men with rifles across the pommels of their saddles and another rode shotgun beside the driver.

Clint smiled grimly to himself. Evidently they had experienced trouble along this trail before. He wondered if the Carswell brothers had anything to do with the protection which had been afforded the stage.

He rolled himself a smoke, lit it and leaned back, resting his shoulders against the trunk of a nearby tree. The stage moved on, out of sight, and silence settled like a growing softness over everything again. In the far distance, the mountain peaks shimmered in the heat, flowing and twisting like molten glass in the air.

He was on the point of whistling the sorrel when he heard the first rumour of another rider on the trail below. Swiftly, he pulled himself upright, peered down through the rising trunks of the trees. The man rode by at a punishing pace, head low over the saddle so that it was impossible to see his face at that distance. It could have been Wingate, Clint decided, returning to Chandler City from wherever he had been. He waited until the solid abrasion of hoofs on the trail had died into the distance before getting into the saddle and continuing along the narrow trail which cut through the timber, over the crest of the hill, down through a deep valley, cut in the rock, where the only pasture was a few scattered clumps of sparse grass and the walls of rock rose sheer on either side of him, hemming him in. Here, he could not see the trail, but there was only the sound of his own mount's hoofs on the hard rock.

Twilight came out of the east and lingered briefly before the full darkness came close on its trail. Clint edged along the overhanging trail, pulling to a walk to give his horse breathing spells. Now that he was approaching Dodge, he suddenly found himself hating every minute of delay and the thought that he might at last, be close on the heels of the men he intended to kill, drove him on and dominated his mind to the virtual exclusion of all else. For the moment, there seemed to be nothing left in him but this one overriding desire to hunt down these men, together or one at a time, however they wanted it, to free himself of this terrible thirst for revenge which seemed to have been the one driving force within him for as long as he could remember.

Perhaps it was this that made him a mite careless as he headed down, out of the timber belt, and on to the main trail into Dodge. The rifle bullet burned along his shoulder a split second before he heard the sharp, flat report. Savagely, instinctively, he hurled himself sideways in the saddle, lying low across the sorrel's back, digging in spurs at the same time. Now he was thankful that he had rested the horse so often during the long, gruelling ride. It responded instantly, bucking a little, then leaping forward as it felt the sharp bite of the rowels in its flesh. Another shot, close on the heels of the first and the slug hummed over his lowered head and lost itself in the dark distance. He had the bush-whacker placed now as the brief flash of the rifle showed for an instant in the darkness. Just off the trail, fifty feet or so, not much further, tucked away in the dark jumble of rocks. There seemed to be only one of them, he decided, but those shots had come just a little too close for comfort.

The impulse to turn, to wheel and head back into the rocks, to hound down the would-be killer exploded inside his mind and body and faded just as swiftly as reason took over control of his emotions. The man was well hidden, could obviously see perfectly in the darkness and could shoot him down from cover quite easily with the longer-ranged weapon.

Nearing a flat stretch of the trail, he gave the sorrel its head, making good ground, listening occasionally for any sound of pursuit, but there was none. Evidently, the bush-whacker did not intend to follow him along the trail all the way into Dodge. The cool night air blew steadily on his face and overhead, the stars shone down brilliantly. He was still high up, even now, and soon came within sight of Dodge. He drifted forward with caution now, still unsure in his mind whether there was a trap being set up for him here and if so, where and when it was likely to be sprung. When he reached the end of the main street of the town, he reined and paused in the dark shadows to take a long look about him.

There was a row of two-storey buildings a little way ahead of him, one of them evidently a saloon with lights pouring from its windows and several horses standing before the hitching rail. For a long moment, he sat there, tall and straight in the saddle, until the sense of wasted time weighed heavily on him. Lowering his hands, he eased the twin Colts slightly in their leather holsters before gigging the horse forward, dismounting in front of a small saloon where there were fewer horses tethered. Thrusting open the doors, he went inside. Six men were seated at one of the low tables playing poker. They eyed him briefly as he stepped inside, then their gaze flickered away and they went on with their game. There weren't any other customers in the saloon and the bartender eyed him with a dead-pan expression on his sagging features.

'Can a man get anything to eat here?' he asked, going up to the bar and leaning elbows on it.

The saloonkeeper nodded dully. 'Reckon I c'n fix you somethin'. Steak and a couple of eggs?'

'Make it three and I'll take it,' said Clint.

The other gave a brief nod. 'Been on the trail all day?' he asked conversationally.

'That's right, headed in from Chandler City. Left this morning at sun-up.'

Two of the men at the table got to their feet, scraping

back their chairs, and moved over to the bar, standing a little distance from Clint. One said harshly: 'If you come from Chandler City, mister, could be you heard about the little fracas there last night?'

'You mean when that rancher band rode into town and started to shoot the place up?'

'That's right,' agreed the other, nodding. His face did not change expression as he went on: 'Jest whose side would you be on if it came to a shooting showdown?'

Clint shrugged nonchalantly. 'Don't reckon I've ever thought about it. Didn't seem to be any business of mine.'

'Could become yore business if you should decide to stop off in Dodge for any length of time.' There was a faint, underlying note of menace in the man's voice that Clint was quick to notice and a little devil dancing at the back of his eyes as he locked his gaze challengingly with Clint's.

'Reckon I'll eat and sleep first before I make up my mind on that.' He held his glass between his hands for a moment, turning it slowly in his fingers, aware of the men watching him more closely than before as if trying to guess at what his next move might be. Plainly there was a little puzzlement in their attitude now, as if they couldn't quite figure him out.

'Don't take too long over it,' warned the second man at the bar. 'Donovan will be itching to tear that town apart after what happened last night. Heard he was lucky to get out of there alive. Those killers and rustlers have been getting things all their own way for too long.'

'I won't.' Clint glanced up as the saloonkeeper came over with a plate and coffee and laid them down on one of the tables on a piece of brown oil-cloth.

Sitting down, Clint found a large piece of steak and the three eggs which the other had promised him. The coffee added its own sharply appetising smell. The barkeep stood hovering on one side as he began to eat.

Between mouthfuls, Clint asked: 'Where are all your usual customers? Surely this place isn't always as empty as this?'

'Most folk eat across the street at the Golden Horseshoe now,' explained the other tightly. 'They don't usually come over here.'

'Any particular reason?'

The other shrugged resignedly. 'Reckon it's because I fell foul of the Carswell boys some time back. They shot up the place twice and since then very few folk have come here. Reckon they're scared of what might happen if they did.'

Clint pursed his lips, bit down heavily on the surge of tense excitement that climbed swiftly through his body 'They're still around these parts, I hear. Has nobody tried to hunt 'em down? Get a posse together and bring 'em in for trial?'

The other laughed shortly. 'You must be a stranger around these parts, mister. Those hills out there are the best part of thirty miles along to the border. You'd lose yourself in there long before you found the Carswell hide-out. Besides if the sheriff ain't in cahoots with 'em, and did bring 'em in, there's no godamned jury in the state would dare to find 'em guilty.'

'So that's how things stand.' Clint grinned tightly. 'And the sheriff – you reckon he's on their side?'

'Difficult to say for sure. He could well be.' The other hesitated, then clamped his lips tight as if suddenly aware that he had probably said a little too much already. He walked back to the bar, then paused. 'You want a bed here for the night too – or were you figuring on going across the street to one of those fancy hotels?'

'Where can a man sleep here?' he asked pushing the empty plate away and sipping the hot coffee.

'I got a big room out back. Town's pretty quiet tonight for some reason. Mebbe something is going to break soon. Sure feels like it.'

The barkeep's words came back to Clint as he sat on the edge of the bunk five minutes later and listened intently to the strange, expectant silence outside that was Dodge. He got to his feet twice, went over to the window, and stared out into the shadows. Nothing moved but somewhere in the near distance, in front of the nearby hotel, a horse whinnied softly, but that was the only sound there was to disturb the night.

The next morning, after shaving in front of the small cracked mirror tacked to the wall of the room, he washed his face and went down into the saloon. The empty tables and chairs had an oddly dispirited look about them that touched him deeply. The barkeep had breakfast ready for him five minutes after he came down. Bacon, eggs and potatoes fried brown. He sipped the coffee slowly, feeling the hot liquid scald the back of his throat. When he had finished the meal, he got up, glanced across at the bartender. 'A mighty fine breakfast,' he said quietly. 'Reckon I'll be checking on the sheriff now, see if he can help me with a little matter.'

'You aiming to stay in town for a while?' The other looked directly at him. 'If so, you're welcome to stay here for as long as you like. Plenty of room now and well – since the Carswells threatened to ruin me and run me out of town, I don't get much custom.'

'This place suits me fine,' nodded Clint. He went to the door and glanced out into the street. Already the heat haze was beginning to dance on the dust. 'Where can I find the Sheriff's Office?'

The other came around the side of the bar. 'Sheriff Varges. First turning on the left, third building along. You can't miss it.'

'Thanks.' He stepped out on to the boardwalk, the tension still taut in him. Around the corner, he found the Sheriff's Office, glass-fronted, the door open. Going in, he found the small, thin-faced man sitting behind the desk. There was a pair of guns on the desk in front of him, the handles towards him. Clint gave them a quick glance, then said tightly: 'Sheriff Varges?'

'That's right,' gritted the other, looking up. His eyes wandered over Clint in swift appraisal. 'What can I do for you?'

'Thought you might be able to help me locate some friends of mine,' said Clint easily. 'Been following their trail from Arizona and across the desert through Chandler City. Heard there that I might pick up their trail here.'

The other leaned back in his chair and a curious expression flickered over his lean features. He placed the tips of his long fingers together, pursing his lips. 'I'll help you if I can,' he said slowly, obviously choosing his words very carefully. 'Just who might these friends of yours be?'

'They call themselves the Carswell brothers,' said Clint evenly.

The other's expression changed swiftly and he half rose to his feet, then sank back in his chair again. 'The Carswells. You a friend of theirs?' Suspicion flared in his tone, backed by vague disbelief. 'Never knew they had any friends.'

Clint shrugged, 'Perhaps they ain't heard about me yet,' he smiled tightly, 'but I'd still like to find 'em, if they are around these parts.'

The other rose heavily to his feet and moved around the edge of the desk. He said slowly: 'Now, listen to me, mister. I'm the sheriff in Dodge. I'm here to keep the peace in this town and the surrounding territory. I don't want any young puppy who fancies his speed with a gun to start taking up against the Carswells. They're bad medicine. You ought to know that if you've followed 'em so far.'

'Then you don't mean to tell me where I can find 'em?' muttered Clint pointedly.

'No. Let's say I'm doing you a favour in letting you stay alive in spite of yourself, besides keeping trouble away from Dodge.'

Clint shrugged. 'Guess I'll have to go out and hunt for 'em myself.' He turned and made for the door.

CHAPTER TWO

BUSHWHACKERS!

Sheriff Varges said in a thin voice: 'Jest a minute, stranger. Reckon I didn't make myself quite clear, If you intend staying in Dodge, I'd better warn you against making trouble. For myself, I ain't seen anythin' of the Carswell Gang. They usually steer clear of Dodge, staying up in the hills. But if you start taking the law into your own hands, I'm going to have to lock you up in jail until you cool off a little.'

Clint stood stiffly by the door, facing Varges. 'Now hold on there, Sheriff.' His lips stretched thin and tight. 'You trying to tell me you're protecting these killers?' He drew in a deep breath, let it softly out. The sudden angry red flush on the other's face told him that the barbed thrust had struck home. But he guessed that this man would not make any issue of it, would force himself to swallow any pride and spark of manhood he had in him. Sheriff Varges, he knew, was not the sort of man to face up to anyone with a gun unless he had a posse of men to back him up. He looked the type to shoot a man in the back or gun him down from under cover.

'That's strange talk from the likes of you,' Varges said finally, swallowing. 'Very strange talk. Now all I'm doing is warning you. Keep those guns of yours pouched while you're in Dodge. I don't want any trouble around here. If you should run into any of those outlaws up in the hills yonder, shoot it out with 'em if you like but you ain't likely to find any of 'em here in town.'

'Is that the usual speech you give strangers in Dodge,' Clint asked harshly.

'Don't be proud of what you reckon you're doing.' The other shook his head, let his gaze fail for a moment to the guns which hung low at Clint's waist. 'They won't help you much if you do bump into the Carswell brothers. Let me give you some advice. Get on your horse and ride out of here, back to where you came from. I've seen dozens of men just like you, thirsting for vengeance, come riding into Dodge looking for men to kill. Up there, on Boot Hill, you'll find that they're still here if you care to take a look – every last one of 'em. They too figgered they were fast on the draw until they met up with the Carswells and a few other outlaws around these parts.'

Clint gave him a prolonged study. The other's remarks interested him rather than angered him and that was a personal reaction to which Clint was not accustomed. It quickened his attention and he watched Varges's face attentively for any sign of a change of expression. But beyond a faint flicker at the back of the watery blue eyes, there was nothing.

'You know, I reckon you worry and talk too much,' he said finally. 'But I'm telling you, Sheriff, I mean to shoot down every one of those crawling polecats I find whether they're on the streets of Dodge or in the hills. And if you or any of your deputies try to stop me, you'll regret it. I know the law as well as you do, and I'm within my rights. All of these critters are wanted in some state or another, dead or alive.'

He expected that would evoke some further reaction but it didn't seem to touch the sheriff at all. His thin tight-lipped smile pushed it on one side. He pulled off his hat, wiped his brow with a brilliant red handkerchief. There were patches of grey around the fringe of his hair and there did not seem to be any immediate danger in this man. But every now and again, a tightness would come into his face and something dark and unholy would flicker at the back of his eyes.

Clint spun sharply on his heel, cut out into the street, his footstep ringing hollowly on the boardwalk before he stepped down into the dust. He was aware of the sheriff's gaze following him, but he shrugged it off and allowed himself to think again of the one thing which had dominated his mind for so long.

Early morning but with the heat haze already beginning to lift. The queer silence that he had sensed the night before was still there, all around him, pressing in on him from every side. It seemed to be an integral part of Dodge, he thought, then caught himself irritably. Maybe the sheriff was right, after all. Maybe it was seldom that any of the Carswell gang came into Dodge. If they stayed most of the time in the hills out there, he might never find them – unless, he reflected, word got around that there was a stranger in town looking for them. He mused on that for a little while, keeping his eyes open.

There was a store directly opposite him and he walked over to it. Just before he reached it, the door opened and two women came out. Clint stepped to one side to let them pass, then stopped dead in his tracks and stared, scarcely able to believe his eyes. The first woman he did not know, thin-faced, angular, with bright beady eyes that watched him briefly from under the poke bonnet as she moved past on the boardwalk with a rustle of black silk. But it was the woman who came out behind her, tall and slim, with dark hair and a roundness to her upper body, who caught and held his attention. She did not look away from his frank stare. She caught his glance and held it with a directness which matched his own, almost a challenging stare, he thought inwardly. She knew she was beautiful and she knew that he had recognized her instantly from the previous night when he had seen her watching him during the fight in the streets of Chandler City. She was a little flattered by his attention and her full lips lay closely together, strangely willful, her eyes wide, cool and appraising. Then she had swept by him, out into the buggy waiting in the street.

Turning away, he went into the cool dimness of the store. There was always the possibility that he might have to head out into the hills and if so, he would need supplies. Inside the store, there was the smell of a hundred things. For a moment, Clint forgot the girl and eyed the man at the back of the counter in surprise. A tall, black-bearded man with shoulders built like those of an ox and a face which seemed to have been hewn from a solid block of granite. He was not Clint's idea of a storekeeper.

'Something I can get you, mister?'

Clint nodded. 'Pound of flour, bacon, jerky beef.' He ran through the mental list of things he would need. While the other was getting them off the shelves, Clint said: 'I guess you get to know most of the folk in Dodge, working in a place like this.'

'Reckon I know nearly all of 'em,' agreed the other. 'This is just about the only store in Dodge and everybody needs provisions some time or another.'

'D'you get many folk here from out of town – from the hills?'

The other paused abruptly, still keeping his back to Clint. There was a sudden tightening of the muscles at the back of of the man's neck, then he said thinly: 'Those goddarned outlaws, you mean, mister? We get them in town now and again, mostly looking for food and liquor, if they ain't looking for trouble. Sheriff does nothing about it, probably too scared to go against 'em, so we have to give 'em what they ask for.'

'I see. Ever get the Carswells in here?'

'Chet and his brothers? Sure – sometimes.' The other turned now and his face seemed to match the colour of the

the flour on his hands. 'You a friend of theirs?'

'Not exactly. But I'm mighty anxious to find them. Any idea where they might be?'

'Guess they could be anywhere.' The dark eyes narrowed a trace. He placed the supplies on the counter, glanced up again as Clint asked: 'One other point. Know a *hombre* by the name of Bart Wingate?'

'Bart, why sure. Everybody knows him. A wild one in his young days, but not since what Chet Carswell did to him. Broke him completely. Now there's a man who should hate the Carswells. If I heard he was out riding after them, I wouldn't feel any surprise, even with that hand of his. But you seem to be a stranger in these parts. Just why are you hunting them?'

'Let's just say there's an old score to settle.'

'With all of the Carswells?'

'That's right. Every last one of 'em.' Clint picked up the provisions, tossed a handful of bills on to the counter. Outside, he started down the street once more in the direction of the saloon. The quietness was still on Dodge and he now had the conviction that if he wanted to find the Carswells, he would have to go up into the hills, try to pick up their trail there and—

The thought was still moving through his mind when a bullet's explosion cut deep into the silence with a shocking abruptness and the scorching breath of it touched him as he caught the movement at the corner of his vision and flung himself to one side, hitting the boardwalk with a blow that knocked all of the wind from his body. The supplies were forgotten, scattered in the dust, as he rolled swiftly to one side, clawing for the heavy Colts. They seemed to leap into his hands as if they possessed a life all their own. He swung himself a little, behind the rail, saw the two men on the far side of the street, crouching low over their guns. Something about them puzzled him. From that distance, they did not seem to be the ordinary type of gunmen. Why then had they opened fire on him like this, like common bushwhackers?

His guns spat lead as he felt the sudden cold hatred pouring through him. Who these men were, he wasn't sure, but they must have had some reason for firing on him without warning like that; and as such, they were lower than rattlers who did at least give warning of their intention. He saw the shape of one of their bodies as the man tried to rise to his feet, clawing for his chest where a widening red stain showed on his shirt. Then he pitched forward over the rail, hung there for a moment, before toppling into the dusty street. His companion, firing blindly now, realizing that they had taken on a rattler by the tail, tried to make a run for it. His feet hammered on the opposite boardwalk as he stumbled forward, firing recklessly. He had covered less than five yards before Clint's bullet took him in the throat.

Slowly, Clint got to his feet, walked out into the hot sunlight, sweeping the slowly-gathering crowd with a quick glance, ready for further trouble. But nobody moved, watching him, waiting for his next move. When he was certain there would be no further trouble, he pouched his guns, moved forward slowly until he stood on the boardwalk, staring down at the nearer of the two men. He lay on his face, on the surface a prosperous man, not a gambler for the clothes he wore were more expensive and less flashy than those associated with such men. But why should men like this try to shoot him down in the street? He surely had no quarrel with them.

Then he put out his foot and turned the body over and found himself staring down into the face of Brad Carswell.

For a moment, the shock held him rigid. Then he found himself able to move again and turned to move across to the second man, lying behind the rail. He did not know what to expect, but before he reached the rail, a voice behind him said thinly:

'Jest keep yore hands where I can see 'em, mister. I don't want to have to shoot you in the back, but I will if you make me.'

Clint stood stock still. He knew without turning that Sheriff Varges would have a gun on him. He wasn't the man to take chances on a straight draw.

'Now turn round, slowly, so I can see you. And don't make any wrong moves.'

Clint turned. As he had suspected, there was a gun in the Sheriff's hand and it was pointed directly at him, the long barrel levelled on his stomach, the finger hard on the trigger. An unpleasant sneer twisted his lips and there seemed to be a look of triumph at the back of his eyes as he lowered his gaze for a moment to glance at the two dead men.

'Don't make a fool of yourself, Sheriff,' Clint said tightly. 'Take a good look at these men. They both jumped me in the street, bushwhacked me. I reckon you might even recognize 'em both. That one there is Brad Carswell. You might find the other is another of the gang. No wonder they decided to shoot me down in the back.'

Varges moved forward, still keeping his eye on Clint, the gun not wavering by so much as an inch. Evidently, he intended taking no chances with a man whose gun was as fast as Clint's. For a long moment, he stood over the nearer body, stared down, his face tight. Clint imagined he saw a sudden flicker of alarm flash across his angular features, but it was gone a moment later and he could not be certain that it had ever been there.

'You're wrong, mister,' he said suddenly, hoarsely, 'Dead wrong. This ain't one of the Carswells. This is Jed Benson. He's well known in Dodge. One of the most respected members of the community. You'll have a hard time explaining this shooting to a jury.'

'A jury.' Clint stared at him, scarcely able to believe his ears. 'I'll tell you that's Brad Carswell. As for the other, I'll bet he's a Carswell too. You trying to cover up for these polecats, Sheriff? Looks mighty like that to me.'

The sheriff grinned mirthlessly. He reached forward, plucked the guns from Clint's holsters, threw them into the dust in the middle of the street. 'Reckon you'd better come along with me, mister,' he said harshly.

'On what charge?' asked Clint stiffly.

The other shrugged. 'Murder,' he said shortly. 'Better move before I forget I'm supposed to uphold the law in this town and turn you over to the townsfolk.'

Clint made to bite an answer, then shrugged helplessly. This had been so clearly set up for him that he doubted if there would be any way out for him. As he turned to walk in front of the sheriff, knowing that it would be useless to attempt to resist or escape, his eyes strayed to the boardwalk a few feet from where the bodies of the two killers lay in the dust. There was an awareness in him, of eyes on him, watching him closely. For a moment, he stared into the sun-thrown shadows, then saw the woman watching him closely, without expression on her face, lips still resting softly on each other. The realization came to him at that moment, that she had seen everything that had happened, that she was a witness to prove that he had killed in self-defence, that those two men had drawn on him first.

The knowledge was a slight easing of the tension within him. Inside the jail, he lowered himself on to the bunk in the corner of the cell, leaned back as Varges locked the door behind him. For a moment, the other stared at him through the bars of the cell. 'Better make yourself as comfortable as you can,' he said a trifle maliciously. 'You'll be there for a little while, until we get the circuit judge around to Dodge. Then I reckon you'll face trial on a charge of murder, shooting down a couple of citizens.'

Clint sighed deeply. 'You know as well as I do, Varges, that those were two of the Carswell gang. I've got a witness there who can prove they shot first.'

The other's eyes narrowed a shade. He thrust out his jaw

aggressively. 'So you got a witness. Mind telling me who he is?'

Clint grinned viciously. 'So you can make sure I don't have one for very long. Is that it?' He shook his head. 'I'll wait until the trial. Then we'll get to the bottom of this. I reckon some folk will want to know why their sheriff is hiding these outlaws, why he won't admit it when a couple of 'em get killed and why he's trying to pin a charge of murder on me for shooting 'em down.'

The other bit his lip then forced a snarling smile. 'You're bluffing.' He spoke as if trying to convince himself. 'If you got a witness, then there ain't nothing for you to worry about, is there?'

Turning on his heel, he walked back along the corridor, slammed a door at the far end. Clint lay back on the bunk, stared up at the low ceiling.

He had no doubts as to the kind of trial he would get once the circuit judge did arrive in Dodge. The sheriff would see to it that everything was tied down as murder. For some reason, known only to himself, Sheriff Varges wanted him dead, would probably have shot him down in cold blood out there on the street had he been certain that he could have got away with it, in the face of the crowd which had gathered. No doubt, already, he would be making the rounds, swearing in as many of the hotheads in Dodge as possible, getting them ready to testify that he had shot first and that those two killers had been decent, upright citizens of Dodge.

Trouble was, he figured, there was nobody here he could turn to. He had even forgotten to ask the storekeeper the name of that woman with the dark hair who had eyed him so directly as she had stepped from the store. He knew that she had been a witness to what had happened. But even so, would that be enough to save him in the face of the overwhelming evidence that Varges was obviously prepared to bring forward? Somehow, he wasn't as sure of himself as he had been a little earlier when the sheriff had first marched him to jail. Then he had been certain that someone must have recognized one of those *hombres* who lay in the dust with his bullets in their bodies. Or were they all so scared of the Carswells that they too, would rather an innocent man hang than come forward and speak the truth at the risk of a bullet for themselves?

Somehow, he told himself fiercely, he had to get out of this jail before the remaining Carswell brothers heard of what had happened and came riding into Dodge, looking for him. Sheriff Varges would certainly not risk his miserable hide to save him from those men. He would either run or hand him over to them without any trouble and once those outlaws got him in the hills, it would be the end of him.

He sucked in a long, heavy gust of wind, tried to marshal the riotous thoughts that spun madly through his mind. There had to be a way out for him, he told himself bitterly. He had come too far, dared too many things, to be baulked at this point. True he had killed two of the outlaws, but that was not enough. He had sworn not to rest until the whole rotten gang of them had been wiped out, and by his gun.

Getting to his feet, he backed over to the solitary window, reached up on the tips of his toes and tested the iron bars set in it. They resisted every effort he made to dislodge them and he knew there could be no escape that way for him. He would have to think of something else.

Varges came along fifteen minutes later with a metal tray and opened the door, stepping through. He set the tray, down and kept a cautious eye on Clint. 'Reckon you better eat up,' he said ungraciously. 'Don't know why I feed you like this. Waste of good vittles. Once Judge Clayburn gets here in a couple of days, it'll take the jury less than half an hour to find you as guilty as hell. Then we'll have to hang you.'

You're making one hell of a mistake and you know it,'

said Clint evenly. His gaze locked with the sheriff's. 'Mebbe you're scared of the Carswells – I don't know. But if that's behind it all, haven't I shown you that they can be killed like any other murderin' polecat? Let me out of here and I'll get the rest of that gang. And you don't have to risk your neck at all.'

For a moment, he had the impression that the other hesitated, as if thinking the proposition over in his mind. Then Varges shook his head. 'You don't trick me that way, Winslowe. I've known those two men for the best part of three years now, ever since they moved into Dodge from back east. If they are two of the Carswell gang as you claim, and I don't believe it for one minute, then you'd better pray that Chet Carswell don't hear about this or he'll come riding into town and take this jail apart stone by stone until he lays his hands on you. When he does that, you ain't going to die easy.'

'So you admit that they were a couple of those outlaws,' said Clint tightly.

'I ain't admitting no such thing,' protested the other. 'I only know 'em by the names they gave when they came here, same as all the other folk in the town. Reckon it'll be up to you to prove that they belong to the Carswell gang and you'll have to prove that you shot in self-defence.'

'Could be I'll do that easy enough,' Clint asserted. 'There must be some people in Dodge who've seen enough violence to last them for the rest of their lives and pretty soon they'll start putting a stop to it. And when they take the law into their own hands, you and the rest of your kind will be finished. That's what you've got to look out for, Sheriff.'

'If that time ever comes,' sneered the other harshly, 'you won't be alive to see it.' He picked up the empty tray and stalked out of the cell, slamming the door behind him and turning the key in the lock. After he had gone, Clint settled himself down on the uncomfortable bunk and tried to sleep. At the moment, there seemed to be nothing he could do but wait for the trial and hope that it would be a fair one. The idea of being strung up after being found guilty of shooting down a couple of the most notorious outlaws in the whole state was too ludicrous for words. Maybe Sheriff Varges was intent on building up a case against him, but provided the judge and the jury were not rigged against him, he felt he had a reasonable chance of getting off.

'All right, Winslowe – on your feet.' Varges's voice cut through the waking consciousness of Clint's mind. He rolled over, then swung his legs to the floor of the cell and stood up. The sheriff stood in the corridor, outside the cell, peering in through the bars. His hand hovered close to the gun at his hip and his eyes never once left the other's face, the expression on his features showing plainly that he was anticipating trouble and hoped that Clint would oblige so that he might use the gun and get things over quickly without having recourse to the coming trial.

Stepping back after unlocking the door, Varges said thinly: 'They're waiting for you over in the courthouse. Won't be long now before you find for yourself how we treat killers in Dodge.'

Clint said nothing. During the past two days, in the jail, he had been able to do a lot of serious thinking. If the trail had been fixed, the jury rigged so that whatever happened, the verdict went against him, then the only chance he would have of escape would be to break from the jail when Varges was in the process of returning him to his cell. It was highly unlikely that they would decide to string him up on the end of a rope right away. Varges would want some little time in which to gloat over his triumph.

They passed through the office door, out into the street. Out of the corner of his eye, Clint noticed that the streets were empty now with only a few horses visible, tethered outside the courthouse and a handful more further down the street outside one of the saloons. Most of the townsfolk, he guessed, would be inside the courthouse, waiting for the trial. He wondered whether the girl would be there, the one person who might be able to save him.

There were two men outside the courthouse. They stood on either side of the door and one of them had just finished his smoke. He ground the butt of the cigarette into the dust under his heel, eyed the sheriff evenly. 'Nobody tried anything so far, Sheriff,' he said evenly. 'Figger that the Carswells may try to ride into town and interfere?'

'There ain't no telling what those outlaws will do,' growled the other. 'Keep your eyes open and let me know the first sign of trouble.' Sheriff Varges swung his gaze in the direction of the four horses tethered outside the saloon. His lips tightened just a shade.

'Any idea whose those mounts are?'

Both men shook their heads as his gaze flicked over them in turn. 'Never seen those horses here before, Sheriff,' muttered the other man. 'Saw the riders come into town, about an hour ago. They stopped off at the saloon and went inside. Looked like strangers to me.'

For a moment, Varges hestitated, then nodded, motioned to Clint to walk ahead of him into the hushed courthouse. As he went inside, Clint stared about him curiously, searching among the faces which turned to watch him. But there was no sign of the girl who had watched him on three occasions, evidently interested in him. His spirits began to sink a little, especially as he noticed the men who sat on the front benches. Evidently they had been hand picked by the Sheriff.

'In there,' Varges interrupted his thoughts. He edged his way into the seat, lowered his body on to the hard surface and waited as the sheriff crushed down beside him. There were a couple of armed deputies standing around the walls of the room and more near the door.

The old laws of the frontier, he thought to himself, never changing. Here there was graft and corruption, with a crooked sheriff and possibly an equally crooked judge. When Judge Clayburn entered and took his place at the table at the head of the room, Clint's suspicions were confirmed. A small, wizened old man, his narrowed beady eyes flickered from one side to the other, before resting on Clint and the sheriff seated beside him.

'This your prisoner, Sheriff?' he asked a trifle testily.

Varges rose to his feet. 'That's right, Judge,' he said quietly. 'Clint Winslowe. He's charged with the murder of two citizens of Dodge, both respected men. Shot 'em down in the street without warning.'

'That's a lie,' snarled Clint harshly, half-rising to his feet.

'Quiet!' snapped Clayburn. 'If you have anything to say in your defence, you'll get a chance to do that before the trial is over.'

Clint sank back into his seat, feeling the grim tightness growing in his body. He could see, even now, how this trial was going to go, what sort of justice he would get at the hands of these men. Probably, he figured, Varges had already been in touch with the Carswells and they were behind it all. Not wanting to come out of hiding, for fear of falling into the trap, they had impressed on him the necessity of having Clint hanged. Knowing Varges, he would never dare to refuse. Even Judge Clayburn was probably acting on orders from the outlaws.

'Very well,' said the judge, nodding. He eased his thin body more comfortably behind the table. 'Let's hear the evidence. We'd better hear what you have to say first, Sheriff, as you made the arrest.'

Varges remained on his feet, a little pomposity in the way he spoke: 'Three days ago, shortly before noon, there was shooting in the street just in front of Jason's store. By the time I arrived on the scene, the prisoner was standing over the bodies of two men who had been shot down from the other side of the street. Neither of the two men had a gun in his hand, although they were both carrying them in holsters.'

Clayburn interrupted drily. 'You're saying that both men were shot before they had a chance to draw their guns?'

'Yes, your honour. I reckon if it had been a straight fight, they would've had their guns drawn when I found 'em.'

The judge made some notes on the papers in front of him, nodding his head with a strangely birdlike motion. Clint sat with his hands clenched tightly in front of him. Slowly, the other was building up the damning evidence against him, and not a single word of it was true. Behind him, he heard the door of the courthouse open, then close as someone came in. Swiftly, he turned his head, but it was merely one of the deputies who came forward and whispered something to the sheriff who nodded quickly, then motioned him out of the courthouse again. He knew now that the girl whose evidence could refute what the sheriff was saying, would not come to give her evidence. For some reason known only to herself, she was deliberately staying away from this place. Perhaps, he reasoned, she did not know that the trial was taking place, perhaps it was impossible for her to come. But even as these thoughts flashed through his mind, a little voice in his brain whispered that if all of these people from Dodge could come to see him tried, surely she could have come too. He sat back in his seat and gave the judge a studying glance.

Slowly, the afternoon wore on. The heat in the courthouse increased as the sun dipped past its zenith. Several witnesses were called to support the sheriff and his story, men who claimed to have been on the scene of the shooting, who had watched him as he had gone for his guns, shooting down the two men in cold blood, without giving them a chance to go for their guns. Out of the corner of his eye, Clint could see that many of the ordinary citizens of Dodge, too, were beginning to believe this story which was being built up against him, a story of lies and half-truths. Once they believed these lies, it would be a short step to a lynching party, organised discreetly and behind the scenes by the sheriff, with the full backing of Judge Clayburn.

They might even try to whisk him out of town under the pretence of saving him from a lynching mob, so that on the way out of Dodge, there would be the heaven-sent opportunity for Chet Carswell and his brothers to get him. Judge Clayburn swung his gaze momentarily towards Clint, watching him with that same expression which had been on his lined, wrinkled features when he had first entered the courtroom – direct and a little speculative, barely showing any interest at all, giving him no hope whatever.

When the last witness for the prosecution had taken his seat again, the judge said harshly, 'Very well, we've heard all of the evidence against this man. I'm sure that every member of the jury has taken full note of it all. Now, we'll hear what the prisoner himself has to say in his own defence.'

Sheriff Varges prodded Clint to his feet. The judge said 'At the beginning of this trial, Mister Winslowe, you claimed that the sheriff was lying. Once we hear your evidence, the jury will decide about that. You claiming that you shot these two citizens of Dodge in self-defence?'

Clint thinned his lips. 'They weren't no citizens of Dodge and the sheriff knows it,' he said, his voice holding a faintly sneering tone. 'They were two of the Carswell brothers, Brad and Bart. Varges here recognized 'em, just as I did, but he's either scared to admit it, or he's in cahoots with those outlaws.'

The judge rapped hard on the table. 'I think I'd better caution you here and now, mister, against making accusations like that against a lawman unless you have proof to back them up. Do you have such proof?'

'Depends on what proof you need,' muttered Clint darkly. 'On the way into the court house, he spotted three horses tethered outside the saloon further along the main street. He has a couple of deputies now, outside the door, on the look out for the Carswells. He seems to think that

44

Chet Carswell and the other two brothers will be riding into town in an attempt to stop these proceedings and take me away by force. Why should he be so certain about that unless he knew that those two men I shot, after they had pulled on me, were Bart and Brad Carswell?'

'You got any answer to that, Sheriff?' asked Clayburn, glancing at the other.

Sheriff Verges said without getting up, 'He's lying, your honour. Sure I have a couple of men outside, but not to look out for the Carswells. I ain't expecting any trouble from them. They won't dare to ride into Dodge in broad daylight for anything. But if this *hombre* has any friends in these parts, they may try to break him out. That's what I'm afraid of.'

Judge Clayburn nodded his head quickly. 'And quite right too, Sheriff. It's always wise to take such a precaution. I'd advise you to stick to the facts, Winslowe, and stop making these false accusations. Now – have you anything else you want to say?' The impatience was clearly audible in his voice.

Clint swallowed. 'Seems like everything has been deliberately set up against me. The jury are all friends of the sheriff's, especially picked. If there are any decent men and women among those present, I reckon it won't be difficult for them to see that I've been framed on this charge. There was a witness at the time of the shooting who could testify that I shot in self-defence, that those two killers drew on me first and bushwhacked me in the street.'

Judge Clayburn nodded his head slowly. 'I've heard from the sheriff about this witness. Is he here in court?'

'It was a woman,' Clint said tightly. 'I noticed her coming out of the store, just as I went in. I don't know her name, but she was in Chandler City that night Donovan's men rode into town and tried to take the town apart. I saw her watching me just after the shooting. She was on the street at the time so she must have seen it.'

45

'And is she here in the courthouse?'

Clint turned his head slowly, then shrugged. 'I guess she isn't,' he said harshly. 'I don't know why, unless someone has got to her already and she's afraid to tell what she knows.'

Clayburn smiled thinly. For a moment, Clint thought he heard a faint ripple of laughter near the back of the court, but he could not be sure. If the ordinary townsfolk were against him, then he stood no chance at all. He tried to tell himself that at the last moment, the woman would show up, but he failed to convince himself.

'You're insinuating that the sheriff here has told this court a pack of lies and that he's responsible in some way for forcing this – hypothetical – witness to remain silent. Is that it?' demanded the other. There was a little snap in his voice and his words were sharp and distinct.

Clint shrugged. 'All I know is that Sheriff Varges warned me against going for the Carswell brothers while I was in Dodge. I got the impression then that he was scared of 'em. Mind you, I ain't saying anything against a man for that. They're one of the meanest bunch of outlaws in this part of the west. But when two of them bushwhack me in the street and I have to shoot them down in self-defence, then I figure something's wrong here when I'm arrested and accused of murder. By rights, I ought to be collecting the reward money for those two polecats.'

Judge Clayburn sighed melodramatically. 'You're not helping yourself at all with these wild accusations. We've heard the sworn testimony of several witnesses, all of them telling the court that those two men you killed were decent citizens of Dodge and that you shot them down, without warning, in the street. That neither of them had a gun in his hand when he died.'

'Then I guess they've rigged this case against me for some reason of their own,' said Clint. He sat down deliberately, noticed the look of annoyance which flashed over the judge's wintry features and felt a little twinge of pleasure, knowing that the barb had struck home.

For a long moment, there was silence in the courthouse, then Judge Clayburn said quietly: 'The jury is now going to retire to consider this case and bring in their verdict. I want to remind them all before they go, that whatever they may think about this case personally, and I know that some of them were friends of the men who were killed, they must put all thought of this out of their minds and ask themselves simply this: Did the accused man shoot them down in cold blood or was it self-defence? If he shot them first, without giving either of them a chance to draw, then it's murder. On the other hand, if as Clint Winslowe says, the two men drew on him first and fired at him from the boardwalk then he had a perfect right to draw and defend himself.'

He coughed once or twice, then went on thinly: 'You've heard a lot about the supposed identity of these two men with members of the Carswell Gang. The evidence given here shows that there was no truth in the prisoner's claim that these men were Bart and Brad Carswell. In coming to your decision, I want you to put that out of your minds completely. Is that understood?'

Out of the corner of his eye, Clint saw the jury nod their heads. Then they went into a huddle, murmuring softly among themselves. He sat taut and straight in his seat, feeling the warmth of the room pressing on him from all sides. The old ways of the west never changed, he told himself, not even here in Dodge where law and order were supposed to be supreme and every man was entitled to a fair trial. But none of those men on the jury would look at this case dispassionately and objectively. Perhaps some of them might be just beyond the law, in cahoots with the Carswells. No matter what the sheriff or the judge said it was obvious that the outlaws were getting help from some of the people in this town and possibly in Chandler City. If they wanted to get rid of him, what better and simpler way was there than to have a few of these men on the jury just to make certain that he was hanged.

The foreman of the jury coughed, then got slowly to his feet. In all, they had talked among themselves for less than ten minutes. He was a tall, lean-faced man with hard eyes that flickered over Clint for a moment before he turned to face the judge.

'Have you come to a decision?' asked Clayburn harshly.

The other nodded. 'We have, your honour. We find Clint Winslowe guilty as hell of shooting down those two men in the street.'

Clint felt the sudden coldness on his face. In spite of the fact that he had been expecting the verdict, the fury with which the other had delivered it, shocked even him. He heard the faint murmur among the rest of the townsfolk sitting at the back of the courtroom, then was hauled quickly to his feet as Sheriff Varges muttered something to the two deputies who sat behind him.

'Clint Winslowe,' said the judge thinly, staring at him. 'You've been found guilty of the murder of two citizens of Dodge. I must say, now that the verdict has been given, that I am in full agreement with it and cannot see how the jury could have brought in any other verdict on the evidence given to the court. There is only one sentence that I can give in these circumstances. You will be taken from here, back to the jail, and lodged there until Friday morning, when you'll be hanged.'

Clint was aware of the sheriff's mocking face looking at him, there was shuffling in the courtroom but very little sound apart from that.

'All right,' said Varges harshly, 'Lets go, Winslowe,' Slowly, Clint walked between the two deputies. It was still a little difficult to believe what was happening. Two of the Carswells dead – and now he was accused of murder and due to hang in three days time. All the way along the street, in the dusty heat and the glare of the sun, he was aware of the faces that watched his every move. There was puzzlement in some of them, and open, frank hatred in the others. The womenfolk watched him with veiled eyes and it was difficult to know what kind of thoughts were running through their minds. Perhaps, he reflected tightly, they were trying to decide for themselves whether that had been a real trial back there in the courthouse, or a farce. If the Carswells had been clever, then it was highly probable that those two members of the gang had worked their way into the confidence of these people, though why, he couldn't figure for the moment. If that were so, then these people, the ordinary citizens of Dodge would not have known the true identities of the men living in their midst and would be prepared to believe everything that the sheriff and his hirelings had said.

Back in the small cell, with the heavy metal-barred door locked behind him, he lay on the bunk with his hands clasped behind his neck and stared up at the ceiling. His mind twisted as he tried to figure things out. Somehow, he had to get out of this jail. Once that was done, he might have a little more time in which to find out what was happening, and an opportunity to discover just where the Carswell gang fitted into what was going on around Dodge and Chandler City.

It was obvious that those two outlaws had known who he was, and had possibly suspected his reasons for being in Dodge. Otherwise, they would not have run the risk of shooting him down in broad daylight. Was it possible that they had been in the midst of planning something and his presence there had thrown all of their plans wrong?

He mused on that for a little while, but got nowhere with such thoughts and finally, exhausted by the heat, fell asleep. He was awakened by the rattle of a key in the lock and a moment later, one of the deputies came in with some food and water which he set down on the floor. As he retreated to the door, Clint swung his legs over the edge of the bunk, sat up and said quickly: 'What's all the hurry? Can you stay and talk for a while? There are a few things I'd like to know and you look as if you might be able to give me some of the answers. They're pretty important.'

'I don't know anything,' muttered the other sharply. His right hand hovered just above the gun at his belt and he was clearly ready for any trouble, obviously suspicious. Perhaps, thought Clint, he had heard of his reputation as a gunfighter and was taking no chances.

Clint shrugged. He noticed that in spite of his suspicions, the other was still inside the cell; close to the door it was true, but waiting. Leaning forward, he picked up the plate and began to eat, watching the other carefully but unobtrusively.

'Those two men they say I shot down in cold blood,' he began, speaking between mouthfuls. 'Did you know either of 'em personally?'

'Nope.' The other shook his head. 'I've seen 'em around often. But for the most part they seemed to keep themselves to themselves.'

Clint nodded, remained silent for a few seconds, then asked: 'You ever heard of the Carswell Gang?'

'Why sure,' said the other. 'They're supposed to be holed up in the hills someplace. There are folk who claim they ride into Chandler City for supplies and some even say that they come into Dodge.'

'And Sheriff Varges. He does nothing to stop 'em when they do ride into Dodge?' Clint lifted his head and stared directly at the other, noticing the faint look of confusion on his face, as if he had said more than he ought to have done.

'We've taken out a posse once or twice to try to hunt them down, but in the hills, a man can lose himself unless he knows them. There are a thousand places for men to hide and the Carswells, like the other outlaws there know every bit of country in that area.'

'So I figured. I reckon then that you never found any of 'em?'

'Never even seen 'em,' affiirmed the other. He leaned against the side of the cell door, still alert, his hand still close to the gun. But he teemed a little more relaxed than before. Clint guessed that Sheriff Varges was not in the jail at that moment, otherwise this man might not have been so free with his information.

'Do you figure I shot those two men down in cold blood?' Clint asked, as he pushed away the empty plate and drank some of the hot coffee.

'Don't much matter to me whether you did or not,' countered the other. 'The jury found you guilty, so there ain't nothing I can do about it. But if those two *hombres* were a couple of the Carswell brothers, then how come the sheriff didn't recognize either of them?'

Clint grinned viciously. 'That's one of the questions I've been asking myself ever since it happened. I know there was no mistake. I've been hunting down that gang for close on five years now. I've hunted 'em across half a dozen states and it wasn't until I reached Chandler City that I finally picked up the end of their trail. When I got to Dodge I asked for the sheriff's help, but he wanted nothing to do with the Carswells. Either he's scared or in cahoots with them. Either way, he probably had to make sure that I was finished, permanently. So he sent word to the Carswells and they laid a trap for me. If that first bullet hadn't gone wild, everything would have gone just as they planned. But I guess they were a little too sure of themselves, wanted to shoot me down in daylight, but they didn't want everybody in Dodge to know what they were doing, or who they were. So they got a little too excited.'

'Makes a good story,' said the other grimly. 'Trouble is that nobody seemed to believe it. You'd have thought somebody would have seen what happened.'

'They did. Only she didn't come forward like I said at the trial. As for those other witnesses – all put up by the sheriff. They said exactly what they were told to say and—'

He broke off as a door slammed at the far end of the passage outside. The deputy stiffened abruptly and stepped away from the door, bent to pick up the empty plate and mug, then stepped outside sharply. A moment later, Varges's voice reached them from along the passage.

'How's the prisoner now?' he called. Clint could hear the sound of his footsteps as he came along the passage. He stopped in front of the cell, then turned to the deputy. 'Better get back into the office Cal. I want a word with this *hombre* in private.'

When the other had gone, Varges stared malignantly through the bars at Clint. That little devil was back again in his watery blue eyes. 'Seems you've landed yourself into a mess of trouble, cowboy,' he said leeringly, and Clint realized that the other was drunk. 'You figured that you could ride in here and shoot it out with the Carswells, but your plans didn't get anywhere, did they?'

'Things ain't finished yet by any means,' Clint snapped back at him. 'A lot can happen in three days as you'll find out.'

CHAPTER THREE

THE CROOKED TRAIL

It was the evening of the following day before Clint realized how quickly things had been moving against him. He had seen the deputy he had spoken to, on several occasions, but the other did not seem to relish any conversation with him now and seemed oddly subdued. There seemed little doubt that Sheriff Varges had discovered that the deputy had been giving away some information and had made it clear that no one was, under any circumstances, to speak to him unless he, Varges, was present.

The day had been unusually hot and sultry with most of the heat somehow filtering through the small window set high in the wall of the cell and once or twice, Clint had imagined he had heard the dull muttering of thunder in the distance, as if there was a storm brewing up somewhere over the mountains. Even when the sun had gone down, there was no change in the exhausting heat and he lay back on the bunk, still vainly trying to figure out some way of extricating himself from this mess, from this trap into which he had walked with both eyes wide open.

When Varges came to his cell that evening, Clint could see immediately that there was something in the wind. The other seemed flushed and oddly elated. He stood just inside the doorway, the shotgun propped against the cell door, within easy reach of his right hand. Curling back his thin, bloodless lips, he said harshly: 'Still trying to figger out some way of beating the rope, Winslowe?' He uttered a harsh laugh. 'Reckon you ain't going to do it, in spite of what you said a couple of days ago.'

Clint held himself in with a supreme effort. 'I ain't dead yet, Varges,' he muttered thickly. 'A lot can happen before you get that rope around me and write me off.'

'Somehow, I doubt it.' There was an odd edge to the other's tone. He seemed to straighten up a little, tensed in spite of his confidence. 'There's been quite a lot of talk in town during these past two days. Reckon some of the leading citizens aren't sure that the law is going to take its proper course. They figure that you may have friends, possibly in Chandler City, and once they hear about you being in jail, they'll ride into town to bust you out. So they've been talking things over.'

Clint ran his dry tongue over his lips. 'And I suppose you've come here to tell me what they've decided to do.'

The other nodded briefly. 'Thought I'd better warn you about the way these people feel. They're stirring up trouble. I can feel it in my bones. Wouldn't be surprised if they don't decide to take the law into their own hands, try to bust you outa here themselves and string you up from one of the nearest trees outside of Dodge.'

'And you'd see to it that they managed to break into the jail without too much trouble,' said Clint grimly.

'Now there ain't no cause to go talking that way,' protested the other, a little too vehemently. 'I've got to uphold the law in this town. And that's what I aim to do. But I've only got four deputies I can call on in trouble like this. We'll hold 'em off as long as we can, but I can't expect any of my men to risk their lives just to make sure that you live for another twenty-four hours.'

'I guess that's putting it plain enough,' Clint shrugged, his mind working furiously. Outside, he heard a muttering in the distance, growing louder gradually as it came nearer. 'The law's dead around here,' he added as a parting shot, for Sheriff Varges had picked up the shotgun and had gone off along the passage.

Clint could not recall when he had felt so helpless. For the hundreth time he tried the bars of the window, but they were of iron and locked securely into their foundations, solid.

Boots thumped on the hollow boardwalk beside the sheriff's office, then faded swiftly into the distance. Relaxing, Clint forced himself to think clearly. Some of the more irresponsible elements in the town had evidently been approached by the sheriff and this hard core of rowdies would be stirring up the rest of the people. It wouldn't take long to inflame them to such a pitch that they came hunting him. A lynching mob was one of the easiest things to get moving, especially in a town like this, with a handful of firebrands to start it going.

Far down the street, there came the sound of harsh voices raised in song, but he could not tell if the sound came from the saloon or the hotel. Wherever it was, the lynching mob was getting itself all worked up on alcohol. There would be a sprinkling of the ordinary citizens of Dodge coming along too, just to make things look legal and possibly to act as a balm to the sheriff's conscience.

'Sheriff Varges,' Clint went to the front of the cell, pressed his face close to the bars and called the other's name along the corridor.

There was silence for a moment, then a man's hoarse voice yelled: 'The Sheriff ain't here. Now shut up your mouth back there.'

It was one of Varges's deputies and Clint tried to recall the man's voice. Outside, along the street, there was more loud talk. A couple of shots were fired, the brief sharp echoes ringing along the front of the street; then he heard the sudden silence which descended on everything. For several moments, he could hear nothing out there, beyond the window. Then there came the slow tread of many men, walking towards the jail, taking their time. The lynch mob was on its way.

'Sheriff Varges!' Standing close to the bars, Clint yelled the name at the top of his voice.

'Now what?' The deputy came along the passage, grumbling harshly. He paused outside the cell, looking in. His face was tight in the faint light, etched with dark shadows. Clint noticed the two guns slung low at his waist. If only he could get the other a little closer to him . . .

'That mob out there,' he said softly. 'I did hear that they were . . .' his voice trailed away so quiet that the other gave a sharp gasp of exasperation and moved closer.

'Speak up!' he ordered roughly. 'If you've got anything to say, hurry up and get it over with. I'm in charge of this place until the sheriff gets back and if there is anything that—'

He broke off with a sudden grunt as Clint's right hand snaked through the bars, jerking the Colt from its holster, levelling it at the other's stomach in one swift movement. Instinctively, the other stepped back into the passage, his hand going for the remaining gun in his belt, then it froze while still several inches above the holster.

'Hold it right there,' snapped Clint harshly, 'unless you want to take the quick trail into eternity. That's better, now unlock the door.'

For a moment, he had the impression that the other intended to make a play rather than let him escape. Then the deputy shrugged, took the keys from his belt and unlocked the door, throwing it open. Very carefully, Clint stepped out, plucked the other gun from the man's belt and motioned him inside.

Reluctantly, the other obeyed. Once he had been bound

and gagged and trussed up on the floor, Clint locked the door behind him, tossed the keys into the cell and ran swiftly along the passage. The sheriff's office was quiet as he went in. There was the remains of a meal on the table, a mug of hot coffee untouched, and a shotgun placed carelessly against the wall. Acting on impulse, Clint snatched it up, checked that it was loaded, then slipped out through the door into the dark street. Thunder rumbled on the horizon, somewhere over the mountains.

Halfway along the street, with the singing breaking out again behind him, almost as if the lynch mob had decided to return to the saloon to build up their courage a little more, a solitary rider turned the corner and rode in Clint's direction. The man was almost level with him when Clint stepped out of the shadows of the boardwalk, the shotgun levelled on the other's chest. 'Off that horse mister,' he said sharply. 'Quickly!'

The other hesitated, opened his mouth for a moment, the jaw hanging slackly open like a fish out of water. Then he slipped from the saddle, keeping his eye on Clint.

'Now move on down the street and keep moving,' Clint snapped, jerking up the barrel of the shotgun threateningly. 'I don't want to have to shoot you down, but I will if I have to.'

'You'll regret this,' muttered the other thinly. 'I know you. You're that *hombre* they arrested and tried for murder a couple of days ago. You don't reckon you'll get very far, do you? They'll have a posse out after you as soon as I give the warning.'

'Better move,' said Clint tightly. 'Before I regret letting you go and shoot you anyway.'

The man turned and began to run slowly along the street, lurching a little from side to side. Before he had gone more than a dozen paces, Clint was in the saddle, urging the horse along the street, towards the trail which led out of town. Behind him, he heard a sharp yell, but it was impossible to make out the words in the peal of thunder which cracked across the heavens.

Until he reached the edge of town, he made no effort to hurry. He did not know how far this horse had been ridden that night and although that posse would be on his heels within minutes of Sheriff Varges getting word that he had escaped he wanted to keep his horse's strength for when it would be really needed. Besides, he told himself, it wasn't Varges and his deputies he was really afraid of, not now that he had guns with which to fight. He had come to shake down things with Chet Carswell and any of his outlaw band still alive and that was what he intended to do.

By the time he hit the trail which led up into the hills, he reckoned that he had a half-mile lead on the sheriff and any posse he had managed to scrape together. The lynch mob, baulked of their victim, might also decide to ride with him, but somehow, he doubted it. Their hatred was not as deep-rooted as to make them come out on a night such as this threatened to be The rain had not yet begun but it was there, in the near distance, drifting steadily nearer, heralded by the vivid lightning flashes which preceded every peal of thunder.

He stayed with the main trail back towards Chandler City for close on two miles, then cut off it, riding up into the timber country on the lower slopes of the hills. Riding into the timber, he increased his lead over the men who pursued him, the drumming of their horses dimly heard in the distance. Not until he reached the end of the timber belt, he and the horse safely screened from the trail below, did he halt and give the horse a blow, narrowing his eyes against the darkness, trying to pick out the first sign of the men who rode after him as they crossed an open patch of ground.

Sheltered by the trees, he was only aware that the rain had started by the faint sound it made as it fell on the topmost branches of the trees. They acted as an umbrella for him, but the men down there on the trail would be drenched to the skin, he reflected. There was a grim, rising sense of amusement in his mind as he sat the horse and waited. They showed up a few moments later. He had increased his lead more than he had realized, but then a solitary rider always seemed to make better time than a bunch of men. The sheriff was easily recognized as he led the men forward. They broke cover between two rising lanes of rock on each side of the trail, a small bunch of riders with a larger bunch following several hundred yards behind. The last group halted in the middle of the open patch and seemed to be talking among themselves for a moment, ignoring the fact that the leading group were still pushing their mounts to the limit, as they set a punishing pace.

After a while, the larger group suddenly turned and headed back into the rocks, going back to Dodge. Clint smiled grimly to himself. Evidently they had decided that it was not worth getting their hides wet just to trail after him, especially as the sheriff did not seem to know which trail he had taken.

He guessed that the sheriff would stick on his tail all through the night. Possibly he had been ordered to make certain that he was dead by the Carswells and he didn't relish the idea of going to them with the news that he had failed, that Clint Winslowe was still alive and very much of a menace to them.

Riding deeper into the timber, he noticed that most of the trees around him were old pines, their trunks stretching up towards the darkened heavens in a flawless sweep, thick at the base and tapering off to where they formed a solid mass of branches and leaves which kept most of the teeming rain off him. There was little underbrush here and he made good progress, the earth muffling the sound of his mount's hoofs. Far away, he could hear the diminishing echoes of the posse as they stuck to the main trail heading

59

east. How long they would ride before the sheriff realized that he had struck off the trail, he did not know. But the sooner he cut up into the hills, the better.

He rode in silence for several minutes, then came out into the open. Leaving the timber behind, he cut across rough country, the rain slashing into his face, half blinding him so that for most of the way he was forced to slit his eyes against it and give the horse its head. Besides, he told himself, in this darkness, his eyesight was of little use anyway.

Presently, he came upon what had once been an old wagon road, leading over the hills, possibly a long-forgotten route into Chandler City. By degrees, the country grew rougher and his progress was slowed almost to a crawl. For as long as he could, he held to the lee of the crests, keeping them between him and the lashing rain, seeking what little shelter he could. The full fury of the storm had now closed in about him and his tunic was clinging chafingly to his skin. Head bowed low over the neck of the horse, he plugged along.

Two miles further on, the horse halted, stood pawing the ground for a moment refusing to budge even when he dug in the spurs. He leaned forward, peering into the blackness, shielding his face against the wind and rain. The horse was tired and seemed doubtful of what lay ahead of it. He had known too many cases in the past when an animal had been able to sense things instinctively, to try to urge the mount forward. Slipping from the saddle, the wind plucking at his body, threatening to sweep him off his feet, rain lashing on top of his head, he edged forward along the narrow, half-green trail an inch at a time. Three yards further on, it plunged down over the side of a precipice where the trail fell abruptly away down the hillside to meet the main trail below. Evidently there had been a recent fault here which had sheared the trail completely at this point, where tons of earth and rock had slid into the valley below. He shivered a little, then edged his way back to where the horse stood patiently, still pawing the ground with its foreleg.

'Looks as if you saved both of us there, boy,' he said quietly. His words were caught and torn from his lips by the rushing wind, blowing straight off the mountains. A tremendous flash of lightning showed him the trail where it fell away in one brief stab of light. Swiftly, instinctively, he narrowed his eyes against it, but he was not quick enough, and for long seconds after that, the night was darker, the blackness more intense than before.

When he could make out shapes again, even though they were but dimly seen, he cast about him, searching for a fresh trail which would carry him further up into the hills. The trail through the timber had been used before, many times, and recently. It might even be the trail along which the Carswells came into Dodge, he mused. Therefore, it meant that there had to be another way up into the hills.

The land around him was deceptive. Turning to the left, he went forward again and less than five minutes later, searching carefully, straining his eyes against the darkness and the rain, ears hurting from the booming thunder which seemed almost continuous now, he found the trail which wound up higher into the mountains, towards the pass which led over the summit, down into the broad, fertile valleys which lay on the other side of the range. It was wild country here, excellent for outlaws, providing them with the virtually impregnable shelter they needed, out of reach of the law.

His horse was tired now and moved forward slowly, head down. Fighting the wind and rain, he tried to make out details of the terrain around him. Several times, he knew that his vision failed him and there was a feeling of uncertainty within him. At the back of his mind, there was also the knowledge that even now, the sheriff and those men who still rode with him, acting on orders to make sure that he was dead, would have realized their blunder and might even at that moment be on the trail at his heels, riding as hard as they dared in an effort to catch up with him before he lost himself in the rough country.

Moments later, he rode between two towering walls of rock which hemmed in the trail on both sides, rising sheer up to the storm-tossed, cloudy sky. They pressed in so close that he could reach with his hands and run his fingers along the rough rock. Here, there was room only for one man to ride. Anyone carrying heavy packs would find it impossible to move along this section of the trail.

By now, his horse was stopping frequently and he began to peer about him, head lowered, in an effort to find some place where he might shelter until the storm blew itself out and he could ride on again. He was not yet safe from the law, and somewhere ahead of him, possibly closer than he thought, the remaining members of the Carswell gang would be waiting, nursing their revenge, ready to cut him down on sight. Or possibly they would wait until they had the drop on him, take him up into the hills, and make sure that he died slowly. He had heard tales of the ways in which these outlaws killed their prisoners. Many such tales had seemed exaggerated at the time of telling, but now, in the thunder-roaring darkness, he was not quite so sure.

It took him the best part of fifteen minutes to ride through the hemming walls of rock, out into the open, where the fierce bite of the wind chilled his body to the bone and his wet clothing flapped about him, beaten down close by the slamming rain which seemed to be beating at him from every conceivable angle.

From the look of the pathway which cut up into the hills, it was little more than a foothold cut out of the solid rock. How his tired, jaded horse managed to keep its balance in the face of the storm fury was something he could not fathom. But somehow, it plodded forward, clearing a sharply-angled bend in the trail. His body felt bruised and raw as he lifted his head and peered through the curtain of rain that poured from the brim of his hat. There, almost directly ahead of him and less than twenty yards away, just on the very edge of his vision, was a darker shape that stood out from the backdrop. Catching up the reins, he urged the horse onward until he drew level with it and saw that it was an ancient, tumble-down hut, possibly belonging to one of the old prospectors who had come to these part, fired with the hope of striking a rich vein and had then departed with all hope crushed and gone.

Dismounting, holding his flapping clothing tightly against his body, he led the horse forward, one hand on the shotgun. There was always the possibility that this cabin was now the hide-out of one of the outlaw bands which infested these hills and after escaping from that jail in Dodge, he did not want to jump right out of the frying pan into the fire, and find himself in the hands of these men. There was not a sound from the place as he approached. Standing for a moment outside the door, he waited for the rumbling echoes of thunder to die away against the hills in the distance, close to the horizon, then pressed his ear close to the wet wood and listened intently. The silence grew thick and huge around him. Finally, he was satisfied. Pushing against the door, he went inside, gripping the shotgun tightly in his fist. The place was empty, rain spilling in through a hole in the roof and splashing against the floor of hard-beaten earth in one corner of the single room. There was the musty smell of dust at the back of his nostrils, and one glance was sufficient to tell him that this particular hut had been deserted for many years. Shuffling his feet forward, he located the table in the middle of the room. Dust lay thickly under his fingers as he ran them over the smooth surface. There were a few mugs and plates on the table, lying where they had been left all those years before. The knowledge that nothing had been touched here for so long reassured him. This seemed just the place to shelter him and the horse until morning; and by that time, he hoped that the storm would have blown itself out, that he would have a chance to get his bearing and start with the serious work of searching for the Carswells. Somewhere along the line, he felt certain he would find the clue which would tell him what was happening around here. More than ever, he felt convinced now that he had stumbled into something big and that his presence back there in Dodge, particularly his killing of those two outlaws, had broken up something really big.

He drew in a deep breath, brought the horse up under the sloping shelter over the small porch, tethered it to the doorpost, although there was little chance that it would wander off during the night with a storm such as this brooding over the hills. Besides, he reflected bitterly, the animal was as tired as he was. All that he wanted now, was to lie down, close his eyes, and sleep.

He made himself up a bed on the floor. The earth felt hard against his back, but he was too tired, too worn out by the experiences of the past few hours to care about that. Pulling one of the blankets he had found in the roll attached to the horse's saddle over him, he listened to the rain drumming heavily on the roof. It sounded like the hoofbeats of a herd of horses in the distance and even as he lay there, half-asleep, he imagined that it was growing nearer, like horses heading up the trail. Once, just to convince himself, he lifted his head from the dirt with a wrenching pull of neck and shoulder muscles, listening intently. But it was nothing more than the rain lashing down from the berserk heavens and he soon settled back again.

When he woke, it was to silence. A deep and clinging silence such as he had known only on the trail, out in the middle of the desert, when he had first ridden into Chandler City. He pushed himself up on to his elbows and stared about him, forgetting for a moment where he was. Then memory flooded back into his mind and he stood up, going over to the door, looking out, back down the trail he had ridden the night before.

His horse was still there, tethered to the doorpost. The storm had blown itself out completely some time in the early hours of the morning while he had slept and now the sun shone out of a cloudless blue sky. He pulled in a deep breath and felt it go down like wine into his lungs. Glancing about him, he noticed the remains of some old mine workings less than thirty yards away. Some time, long ago, possibly before the war, he thought, someone had come out here, away from civilisation, shutting himself off from his fellow beings, hunting through the dirt for the precious metal which was to have made him rich. He doubted whether that man, whoever he had been, would have struck it rich. The area had been full of prospectors in those days, each man convinced that he would be the lucky one. And those who did strike gold, lost it all in the saloons down in Dodge and Chandler City, lost it to the crooked gamblers, the card-sharps, or to those who were less subtle and took it from them at the point of a gun.

As he stood there, he deliberately forced away the gnawing hunger pains in the pit of his stomach. The ground around him was steaming as the heat of the sun, growing stronger with every passing minute, sucked all of the moisture out of the soil.

Somewhere around here there would be a stream, he told himself. None of the old prospectors ever camped very far from one. Water was the one thing they could not do without. Loosening the rope, he led the horse forward, down the slope, skirting the old mine workings. A few moments later, he found the stream. Swollen a little by the heavy rain of the past few hours, it raced over rounded, smooth stones. He let the horse drink its fill, then drank himself, before filling the empty canteen. His face and neck felt sticky with the sweat and he splashed the water against his head, feeling the coldness of it shock some of the life back into his body.

It was as he got to his feet that he heard the new noises in the sunlight. They seemed to be murmuring from somewhere close at hand, but after a moment's pause, he realized that they were being carried down by the stream and that whoever it was who was talking was still some distance away. Waiting and listening, he tried to make out the words, but they were muffled by the intervening distance and he could only hear snatches of the conversation. None of the voices he recognized.

Creeping back to the horse, taking care not to make a sound just in case it also travelled back along the surface of the water, he reached the horse, swung himself up into the saddle. The day which stretched ahead of him seemed bleak. He had to get through this country, possibly back to Chandler City if he could not locate the Carswells. At least, somewhere in Chandler City he might find that girl who could clear him. But there was to be no breakfast, no midday meal and there was not even the chance of any supper in sight at that moment. He gigged the horse forward at a slow trot, holding his breath involuntarily at the sound of its hoofs on the hard rock, ringing like metal on metal. Oh God! he thought inwardly, surely that sound must have carried to those men in the near distance.

He drew in a huge breath, then let it go. Crossing the stream, fording it easily in spite of the wave of swollen water that rushed down on them, he hit rock country ahead, paused until he had travelled the best part of a quarter of a mile, then gave the horse its head. Freshened after the night's rest, it responded gallantly, running sure-footed between the rocks.

What warned him that there was trouble directly ahead, he did not know. But the warning rang in his mind and he reined the horse swiftly, almost savagely. It reared up on its hind legs and as it did so, he caught a glimpse of the solitary rider who sat motionless in the saddle, among the trees which bordered the trail some thirty yards ahead. For a moment, he thought that the other had not seen him, but a second later, he caught the movement as the man brought a rifle up to his shoulder and fired in almost the same instant.

The bullet hummed dangerously close to Clint's head, striking the rocks behind him, wailing off thinly into the distance. In a single fluid movement, Clint swung himself out of the saddle, behind the horse, tugging hard on the reins until it moved into the lee of the rocks. The man ahead of him had an excellent position, well back among the trees where they grew in a small clump close to the trail. From there, he could fire almost directly along the trail without exposing himself to much return fire.

He rolled away from the fire as a second bullet smashed against the rock where his head had been a few moments earlier. The horse was a couple of yards away, still near the trail and the shotgun was in the scabbard. At the moment, this was the only weapon with the power to reach that man and he knew that he had to stop him before he could summon any others to the scene.

Taking a swift look around the edge of the rock, he chanced a glimpse in the direction of the outlaw. He could just see the other, fumbling with the rifle. Lurching to his feet, he darted out into the open, reached up for the shotgun as the horse bucked and shied away from him. A couple of bullets struck the ground at his heels as his fingers tightened on the gun, pulled it free of the scabbard and then rolled back under cover.

Even crouched behind the rocks, his vision was too limited. To see the other and get in a killing shot, he would have to lift himself out from behind cover. Gritting his teeth, he grasped the shotgun tightly in his hands, waited while the other loosed off another couple of shots, then jerked himself upright, aimed swiftly, and pressed the trigger. The gun bucked strongly against his shoulder, knocking the wind from his chest. For a moment, it seemed that, even with this weapon, he had missed. The man seemed to have edged a little further into the open just at the moment that he had pressed the trigger. Then he saw that the other was swaying clumsily on his feet, that the rifle was no longer in his hands but had fallen from fingers suddenly nerveless. For a moment longer, the outlaw remained on his feet, then he toppled forward as if suddenly struck in the back by an invisible fist, hit the edge of the rocks overlooking the trail, and rolled down to land with a thump among the boulders.

Clint took his finger from the trigger and rubbed his shoulder where the butt of the gun had thumped against the flesh. Cautiously, he went forward until he stood over the man. Going down on one knee, he turned him over. The shotgun had done its work only too well. No man could have lived for more than a few moments with those wounds. Exhaling slowly, he got to his feet and stood stock still for a while, listening intently. The timberland around him was quiet. In the distance, he could hear water running, but that was all. There was no indication that this man had not been alone in this neck of the woods.

Going back to where the horse stood on the trail, he leapt into the saddle, kicked it forward with a dig of the spurs. The shooting might have been heard by anyone in the vicinity and he wanted to be well away from there before they came looking. He ran the horse along the trail for perhaps a mile before easing it back into a trot, allowing it to blow freely. The pangs of hunger were beginning to gnaw more strongly at his stomach and it was impossible to ignore them altogether. When he glanced back over his shoulder he saw that he was sheltered from the trail behind him. In front, there was a rough slope, but it was a passable one and he took it slowly. At the moment, he had no clear idea of his future plans. These hills were outlaw country, but there was no sense in riding up to the pass and moving over them into the valleys beyond. He still had a job to do and he meant to do it to the best of his ability. Two of the Carswells were dead, struck down by his own gun. That meant three more to go, including Chet, the leader of the gang.

He crossed another river half a mile further along the trail. The river had been born in these mountains and although it travelled swiftly between rocky banks, it was shallow, easily forded, though breaking hard against the horse's forelegs. On the other side, the country was more rugged, but more open. He was skirting the eastern side of the mountains. Pines grew tall in places, but the patches of timber were more isolated, more widely spaced than they had been earlier, which meant that anyone on the look out for him could spot him over much longer distances. Gently, he eased the Colts in their holsters. They were poor weapons for long range work, and he guessed that the sheriff and his men, if they were still on his trail, still hunting for him in this wilderness of rock and pine, would be carrying rifles. Varges was no fool and he would have realized at the outset that if Clint once made into the hills, a rifle was the only weapon which could smoke him out.

A little before noon, with the sun blazing down from the cloudless, flat mirror of the sky, he paused in a small hollow. Dismounting, he stretched his legs, easing the cramp pains which had been troubling him for the past hour. The horse had been struggling with the slippery, treacherous rocks during the last part of the climb, striving to keep its balance, working through the huge boulders which blocked their view whenever they passed between them.

He seated himself on the top of a low, flat rock and studied the terrain around him. This was all unfamiliar country as far as he was concerned and he was acutely aware of the fact that he could be jumped at any moment by the outlaws. How long he had been sitting there before he heard the sound, it was impossible for him to estimate. At first, it was so faint that his tired mind tended to disregard it. Then he forced himself to listen and picked it up instantly, recognizing it at once. He got swiftly to his feet, passed around a huge chunk of smooth rock and peered down the steep slope. He spotted the riders almost at once, mere specks against the valley floor.

There were half a dozen of them at least, but from that distance, it was impossible to tell whether or not it was Sheriff Varges and the posse, still determined to track him down no matter how long it took. Clint grinned slightly to himself, feeling the grim amusement in his mind. At least Sheriff Varges was probably the one lawman who could ride through this country without being afraid of an outlaw bullet in his back the moment he showed himself. He was probably on nodding terms with all of the polecats in these hills, tipping them off whenever there was likely to be any trouble in Dodge or Chandler City, or when there was a gold shipment moving through on the stage.

He watched them closely for a long moment, studying their movements. In a little while, he knew that they were moving off the trail, up into the rocks. He saw the man in the lead throw his arm up in the direction of the summit, almost directly to where Clint lay behind the rock. He lay very still, feeling his danger. If those men did ascend that trail and begin to search for him, spreading out in a long line, it was only a matter of time before they ran him to earth. And there was also that dead outlaw back there on the trail, evidently looking for him, who would soon be discovered. Caught between two groups of killers, he would stand very little chance in this wild country.

Swiftly, he turned to examine the trail above him. It wound up the side of the hill until he lost it among the tumbled heaps of boulders near the summit. He turned to go back to the horse, then stopped, right hand clawing for the gun at his waist, cursing himself for not having realized that danger could come from two sides, and that while giving all his attention to the men down below, he had forgotten about the trail along which he had just come.

'Relax, Winslowe.' The voice stopped the downward

motion of his hand. 'This is a friendly call.'

Clint noticed two things within a split second of each other. The fact that there was no gun in the other's hand, and that the right hand, ungloved, was all twisted and clawed.

'Bart Wingate.' He pushed himself to his feet, taking care not to lift his head so that he might be seen from below. 'What the hell are you doing here?'

The other grinned. There was a curious, vicious expression on his lean features. 'Might ask you the same question,' he said, squatting. 'Figured you would head this way once you busted out of that jail in Dodge. Yeah, I heard all about that and came after you as soon as I could. Reckoned that, since you don't know these parts at all, you might get yourself lost – or worse still, picked up by the Carswells.' His voice tightened a little towards the end and he sat hunched forward over the rocks, taking off his hat and running the back of his hand over his forehead. He squinted up at the sun for a moment, then walked forward and glanced down into the valley, around the edge of the flat-topped rock.

'They don't seem to be in any hurry to come up here and git you, do they?' he remarked. 'I gather that is Sheriff Varges and some of his hired killers down there on your trail.'

Clint nodded. 'That's right. They've been tailing me since dark last night. I holed up in an old shack until daybreak then headed up this way. I figured I might be able to lose them in the rocks, then either go after the Carswells or head back into Chandler City. There's a woman there who knows I didn't shoot down those two men in Dodge in cold blood.' He paused and glanced keenly at the other out of the corner of his eye. 'Reckon you heard about that fracas in Dodge. They got me framed on a charge of murder. Sheriff Varges brought in half a dozen of his own men to swear they saw me shoot down two honest, decent citizens in cold blood. They were going to hang me today.'

71

'You know who those two *hombres* were that you shot?'
Wingate looked at him queerly for a moment, the sunlight
etching his face with shadow.

'Sure. A couple of the Carswell brothers. I recognized
'em both. Bart and Brad. Sheriff Varges swore they were
men who'd lived in Dodge for a year or so. Honest-to-good-
ness citizens.'

Wingate tightened his lips. 'To most of the townfolk in
Dodge that's exactly what they were. Prosperous men who
never interfered in the running of the town. But they were
there for a purpose.' He came back and sat down. 'Those
men down there won't get here for another couple of hours
yet,' he said easily. 'And in this heat, it ain't going to be a
comfortable ride for any of 'em.'

Clint scowled. 'You got any food with you?' he asked. 'I
never felt as hungry as this before, not even in the desert.'

'You'll find something in the saddle-bag,' nodded the
other jerking his thumb towards the horse which had been
tethered several yards back along the trail. No wonder he
hadn't heard the other come up on him from behind,
thought Clint. Thank God that it hadn't been one of the
Carswells or he would have been dead by now. There was
bread and a hunk of cheese in the bag and he took it out
and ate ravenously.

Wingate turned from his position near the rock. 'They're
more than a couple of miles down the trail,' he said casually.
'Making pretty slow progress. That trail there ain't been
used much for the past ten years to my knowledge. I reckon
Varges will be cursing plenty by the time he gets to the end
of it.'

'And where will we be by that time?' asked Clint directly.

'Reckon we could be anywhere,' muttered the other.
'Depends on what you've figuring on doing. Wouldn't
advise you to ride after the Carswells alone, not right now.
They know that you've busted out of jail and they're ready

for you. They could shoot you down before you knew they were there. Just as I could have a while back.'

'Guess you're right. What do you figure I ought to do? I can't go back into Dodge, that's for sure. And they'll have wanted posters up for me all over the state by now. Varges isn't going to rest until I'm caught and no sheriff or ranger is going to stop and ask himself whether Varges is in with these outlaws, before he shoots me on sight.'

'There ain't any real law in Chandler City. Not right now, anyway, though it might come soon. You'd be safe there until you'd had a chance to clear yourself. Besides, there's somebody around here who's mighty interested in you.'

'Chet Carswell?' asked Clint bitterly.

'Nope. Donovan, the rancher. Sure, he rides into Chandler City on occasions and shoots the place up with some of his men. But he's straight and he listens to no sheriff. If he takes a liking to you, then there ain't nobody who'll take you off his ranch.'

'Why should he do that for me?'

Wingate shrugged. 'I've really no idea. Probably he figures that you're the type of man we need around here. In these parts, everybody either crawls to the outlaws in the hills – and that means Chet Carswell – or tries to line up with those men in Chandler City. The gunslicks and gamblers. Either way, they're against Donovan and a small bunch of ranchers who're trying to make something of this country, something good and lasting and decent.'

Clint looked at the other in surprise. 'I heard back in Dodge that you used to belong to the wild bunch, before – well, before Chet did that to you.' He glanced towards the other's right hand.

Wingate looked at him directly. 'All that's in the past,' he said, musingly. 'Funny thing, when you're young you live by the gun and more often than not, you die by it. I'm a lot older than you. I've seen what lawlessness and outlawry can bring to a country that's struggling to grow up and stand on its own two feet. There's only misery for men like that and sooner or later, this country has got to drag itself out of lawlessness if it's to survive. This is no good, what's happening now. Crooked sheriffs like Varges, working in cahoots with the killers in the hills. Bad years when there's only the smell of gunsmoke over the country and men die suddenly and without knowing what they're dying for.'

I see.' Clint could think of nothing else to say. He got to his feet, went over to the rock and stood, looking down at the small group of dark figures as they toiled up the steep, rocky slope in single file. Their horses were obviously tired and it was possible that Varges had forced them to travel through the night with very little rest, his fierce hatred and hurt pride pushing him on. He saw Varges halt and glance down at the trail, evidently trying to pick up any tracks, but although he clearly found none, he continued to lead the men forward, occasionally pausing to glance up towards the summit, shading his eyes against the glare of the sun.

Wingate got up and came over to stand beside him. 'Another hour or two,' he said casually. 'We might be able to drop a few of them from here when they get closer. But the firing could bring the outlaws down on our necks and we couldn't tackle them alone.'

Clint hesitated, then nodded. For a moment, the thought of killing Varges had been uppermost in his mind, dominating his thoughts. Then he forced himself to relax. That would solve nothing at the moment and could, as Wingate said, land them in a lot more trouble.

'Let's go,' he said shortly. 'We won't make Chandler City before dark anyway. We may have to hole up somewhere through the night.'

The trail lay upgrade for five miles or more and throughout the long, hot afternoon, they made a series of sharp turns along the trail, Clint following close behind Wingate, trusting him to find their way out of the hills. At times they moved across a multitude of narrow tracks and for the first time, Clint realized that he would have been completely lost had it not been for this man who seemed to know every trail in the mountains, whose uncanny knowledge and instinct picked out their trail instantly from the rabbit warren of narrow tracks which ran in a maze in all directions.

Soon, as they rode, their shadows lengthened and fled in front of them. The pursuit seemed to have difted away in the distance behind them and it was pretty obvious that Wingate had given the sheriff and his posse the slip among the rocks and by the time the sun was touching the rim of the horizon, they were among timber country once more, in terrain which was more open than before. Ahead of them, as they swung in a wide circle to skirt the upthrusting outcrop of rock which marked one end of the mountain chain, there was a great burst of flame from the western horizon as the sun went down in a sudden blaze of glory. For a moment, the sky held the redness, the deep gold of the sunset, like a last lingering echo of some gigantic fire. Then the glow faded with an incredible swiftness and the land around them, the whole countryside changed. It became a cooler, blue world where the shadows were dark patches of indigo and the valley which lay in a broad sweep below them was filled with various shades of blue and purple as the night came.

Only high above them, where the mountain peaks thrust themselves up into the sky, was there any last, lingering touch of redness, as the dying rays of the sun drifted over the crests of the mountains, lighting them for a brief moment before that too faded.

'Be completely dark soon,' muttered Wingate. 'More than ten miles yet to Chandler City. Reckon we'd better do like you said a while back and make camp for the night.'

'Think we can risk a fire?' asked Clint, reining his mount to a halt. 'Or are we likely to run in with those outlaws out here?'

'That ain't likely,' the other replied, sliding from the saddle. He took the reins and led his horse forward a little way, standing on the very edge of the trail, looking down. 'We're in pretty open country here and they won't be riding this close to the main trail, unless they catch up with Varges and his bunch and hear from him that you're somewhere in these parts probably heading for Chandler City. If that happens, reckon we'll get plenty of warning of their presence.'

He came back, tethered the horse to an upthrusting tree stump and motioned Clint to get down.

'Where will that trail they were on lead them eventually?' Clint asked, turning his head and peering back along the trail.

Wingate swung an arm to the north, back towards the looming hulk of the mountain. 'If they follow it all the way, they'll go clear up to the summit and Saddlehorn Pass. It ain't likely they'll go over the top. You'd be a pretty poor fool to do that. Varges will know by now that you ain't so hellbent on getting out of the area as to ride across the mountains. He'll realize you'll probably try to carry out your threat of killing the rest of the Carswells and I reckon his first act, when he realizes that you've slipped through his fingers will be to warn Chet that you're free and hunting him.'

The other paused, then glanced about him, moving off into the trees. Clint heard him hunting around for a little while, then he came back with an armful of dry twigs. Placing them in the middle of the small, circular clearing in the rocks, he struck a sulphur match, put light to them, and squatted back as they blazed up, throwing a wide circle of light in the darkness.

CHAPTER FOUR

OUTLAW BREED

Clint sat with his feet towards the fire, staring across through the flames at the man who squatted opposite him. A man with hatred still burning fiercely in his heart, although he professed that he was all for the country growing up and forgetting its old ways of violence. But perhaps, Clint reflected, the memory of what Chet Carswell had done to him was still ingrained too deeply on his mind for him ever to forget that and he would not rest until all of those men had died by the gun or were dangling from the end of a rope. Perhaps then, and only then, he would feel clean and free again.

As though feeling the other's reflective gaze on him, Wingate lifted his head, the firelight playing on the greying hairs at his temples, lighting up the dark eyes.

'You still wondering why Varges turned against you, Clint?' he asked in a soft, amused voice.

'Some,' agreed Clint stiffly. 'Seems he had me picked out the minute I rode into town.'

'Did you tell him you were looking for the Carswells?'

'Yeah. I asked if he knew where I could find 'em, told him that somebody had seen 'em around Dodge. He warned me against looking for them in town, said that if I persisted in looking for trouble, he'd have to take away my guns so long as I was there.'

Wingate nodded. 'When you rode into Dodge, did you take the main stage trail?'

'No. I followed it for a couple of miles or so and then cut into the timber. Wasn't sure whether or not there was somebody tailing me.'

'And was there?'

Clint nodded grimly. 'Somebody headed into Dodge, pushing his horse to the limit. Then somebody tried to take a shot at me from the rocks just before I reached Dodge.' He paused, then felt a sudden tightness grow within him. Each of these little events, which at the time had seemed entirely disconnected, now began to slot themselves together in his mind, to form a picture which was beginning to make sense. A crazy kind of sense, it was true, but the more he thought it over in his mind, the more feasible it seemed.

Wingate nodded as though divining his thoughts. 'Somebody seemed mighty anxious to let Varges know you were headed for Dodge,' he said softly. 'It could only have been somebody who saw you in Chandler City. Did you recognize the rider?'

'Couldn't see much,' admitted Clint grudgingly. 'But why should anybody take all this trouble to inform Varges – unless they were in cahoots with Carswell and wanted Varges to get me out of the way before I started too much trouble.'

Wingate did't seem to have heard the last part of what Clint had said, for he went on quickly. 'You couldn't tell then if it was a man or a woman you saw riding hell for leather into Dodge.'

Clint sat stiffly upright by the fire, felt the sudden rush of coldness to his face as the implications behind the other's question hit him with the force of a physical blow. 'A woman!' He jerked the words out from between compressed lips. 'You're not saying that—'

Wingate shrugged. 'I ain't saying anything,' he muttered. 'But it does seem odd that the one person who could clear your name, who's obviously been taking plenty of interest in you since you rode into Chandler City, never turned up to give evidence on your behalf when you were on trial for your life.'

'But why should she – No, I don't believe it. There was no reason for her to do anything like that. Besides, what would she have to gain by allowing an innocent man to be hung, just for shooting down two rats like that?'

'That's something I don't know, and neither do you. Reckon you'd better find out soon though.'

'You got any ideas?' asked Clint sharply. 'You must have, or you wouldn't have suggested that she had anything to do with this.'

'Could be.' The other fell silent for a long moment, staring into the fire. Then he said softly: 'Those two men you killed in Dodge. Why do you reckon they were there, masquerading as prosperous citizens, using false names?'

'Suppose you tell me.' Clint shifted his body into a more comfortable position and held out his hands towards the fire as the cool night air flowed about him.

The other leaned back. 'You heard of the San Miranda Mining Corporation? It operates a little to the west of here.'

'Vaguely. It's a gold mining concern, isn't it?' Clint felt puzzled. Just what had a corporation like that got to do with the Carswells?

'That's right. Occasionally, they ship gold through the state to the east. Usually it goes by railroad with plenty of armed guards to make sure that it gets through. But there has been talk that a shipment is going through by stage and that means it will have to pass through Dodge and Chandler City. There'll be close on half a million dollars' worth of gold in that shipment. A worthwhile prize to any outlaw gang, wouldn't you say?'

'And you figure the Carswells have been planning to take

79

the stage carrying that bullion?'

'It figures. But first they would have to get some valuable information, when the stage will pass through here on its way east. How many armed guards will be travelling with it. And probably most important, whether they'll be pushing through a dummy stage with nothing more valuable in it than a few sacks of stones. That's why Bart and Brad Carswell were in Dodge, why they've been there for so long, masquerading as prosperous citizens, to get this information and relay it back to Chet up in the hills.'

'And of course, they'd have to have the sheriff in on the deal too. He'll get some of the advance information which he could give to them.'

'Right again. Now maybe, you see where you fit into the deal. You could have made things hot for these outlaws if you weren't stopped. So the order went out that you were to be killed, shot down in Dodge. Trouble was, you shot first, killed both of the Carswell brothers before they could tell what information they had. Whether you know it or not, I figure that you've foiled one of the biggest stage holdups in the history of this state. Can you blame Chet for feeling sore? Not only have you killed two of his brothers, but you've robbed him of the chance to get his hands on half a million dollars of gold.'

'Do you know if that stage has gone through yet?' asked Clint.

'Could have. But nobody seems to know for sure, except the gold mining people and they won't talk.'

'So for all we know, Chet and his men may still be preparing to take that gold.'

'If they do, they'll be still working in the dark. Those mining corporations are not fools. They'll have heard of the Carswells and they'll know the dangers of shipping it through this territory.'

Clint lay back on the hard rock and drew in a heavy breath. There was no wonder that Varges had been so determined to have him strung up, even to the point of deliberately framing him with murder once Bart and Brad Carswell had failed to kill him. Then, when there was the possibility that he might be broken out of jail, Varges had stirred up some of the roughnecks in Dodge, getting a lynching mob together, no doubt going out into the town and making sure they finished their job.

'Reckon we'd better get some sleep,' said Wingate finally, his voice soft in the darkness which lay beyond the glow of the fire. 'Let the fire die down. If they do pick up our trail, we ought to get enough warning to be ready for them.'

Clint nodded, lay back and pulled the blanket over his body. For a long while, unable to sleep, he stared up at the sky over his head where there was a bright powdering of stars. The moon was low on the horizon, only a thin crescent now, giving little light. Now that he knew a little of what he had ridden into when he had come to this territory seeking revenge on the Carswells, it was possible to begin to plan ahead, to work out what he was going to do. But even as he lay there, he found his thoughts beginning to stray more and more, to that dark-eyed woman who had watched him directly on so many occasions. Surely, he told himself fiercely, there could be no truth in Wingate's supposition that she had been the one behind this attempt to kill him out of hand. But someone had ridden hard from Chandler City into Dodge that same day that he had taken the trail, ridden in so as to warn Varges. There was no longer the slightest shadow of doubt about that in his mind now.

He tried to think back to the figure he had seen on horseback, riding swiftly along the trail into Dodge. Could it have been a woman? From that distance it had been impossible to tell and looking back he had to admit to himself, however reluctantly, that it could have been the girl he had seen – it could have been she who had fired on him as he had approached Dodge. He reviewed what had happened in the past few days, trying to plan the best course open to him. He was still as determined as ever to hunt down the Carswells and see them in hell before he died himself. As for Sheriff Varges, he might have to kill him too and those men who rode with him.

As he lay there, on his side, with the blanket over him, he found his thoughts turning to Donovan, one of the most powerful men in the territory, and if Wingate was to be believed, one of the few straight men who seemed to have dedicated himself to erasing outlaws and their memory from the area. But Clint had seen what had happened in Chandler City. On that particular occasion, Donovan had been lucky to have escaped with his life. Perhaps he was beginning to realize, even now, that the odds were stacked too highly against him.

After an indeterminate time, he fell asleep, only to waken while it was still dark, dragged from the depths of an exhausted doze by someone shaking him violently by the shoulder. Opening his eyes, he saw Wingate bending over him, speaking to him urgently.

'Wake up. Clint. Posse headed this way.'

Within seconds, he was wide awake, forcing away the exhaustion which still clawed at his body, aching limbs moving as he pushed himself upright. 'Where are they?' he muttered hoarsely, peering into the darkness.

It still wanted a couple of hours to dawn and the stars were still bright where they stretched clear across the dark heavens. In his ears, he heard the faint sound of approaching riders, but for the moment, newly wakened from sleep, he could not tell from which direction they were coming.

Wingate said swiftly, urgently: 'They must have decided to try to box us in. They've cut behind us – at least their main force has and they're coming down fast from that old Indian trail up to the summit. They'll be on us in less than fifteen minutes.'

'Then there's no time to run,' Clint whispered. He pulled both Colts from their holsters, checked that every chamber was loaded, then slipped them back again. 'We'll have to take 'em from here. Think you can handle a gun?'

'I guess so.' There was no expression in the other's voice. His mouth was tight as he edged towards the rocks which lifted clear on the edge of the wide circular clearing. 'They'll come riding down that trail there. We'll see 'em before they get within range. But if they have rifles, we'd better let them come in close, all of them, before we fire.'

'That makes sense,' agreed Clint. He wondered for a moment about the shotgun, then realized that he had no more ammunition for it. Crouching down behind the rock, he tried to make out shadows along the trail that stretched away in front of them, climbing steeply to the summit.

'They seem to be making plenty of noise,' whispered Wingate. He turned his head, cocking it a little on one side in an attitude of listening. 'They can't know that we're here or they wouldn't signal their position like that.'

'Here they come.' Clint touched the other on the arm, nodded in the direction of the trail. He could just make out the shapes of the riders as they came out of the shadows of the rocks, cutting down the trail, the horses picking their way carefully among the scattered boulders. The men seemed to be lolling in their saddles, tired men he guessed who had ridden far and ridden hard. Men who could scarcely keep their eyes open. They would have been on the trail all that day, through the terrible glaring heat of the sun during the day and now in the bitter, cold wind that blew down the slopes.

Clint tightened his lips. There was no feeling in him at that moment, as he crouched there, knowing that he held the lives of all these men in the palm of his hand at that moment, that he had only to lift his guns, wait for a few more moments until they came within range, and half a dozen men who knew nothing of it, would die as they rolled out of their saddles.

Half-asleep, they were not alert. They made a pretence of

searching the territory to their right and left, but most of them saw little and what they did see, registered sluggishly on their tired minds. It was going to be like shooting sitting ducks, he thought dully. But every one of these men would do the same if the positions were reversed and it was he who rode into a trap. He felt no pity for any of these men. Confirmed killers, they followed Varges because they wanted to, because shooting and killing and violence were part of their nature. *Those who live by the gun, shall die by the gun*, he thought savagely.

The riders came on unknowing of their danger. They were now close enough for him to recognize the man who sat in the saddle on the lead horse, the only man who sat upright, all the rest dragging forward over their pommels. Sheriff Varges. There was no mistaking the other.

Clint shrugged mentally. Well, perhaps there was a little courage in the man, he reflected, to make him ride the trail like this, with something driving him on all the time. Or was it courage? He knew nothing of what lay just ahead of him. As far as he was aware, these hills were country that belonged to the outlaws and as far as most things went, they could be counted among his friends.

No, it wasn't courage that had made him ride through the hell-heat of the day, the dust and the fies, into the dark coldness of the mountain night. It might even have been fear that was driving him. Fear of what might happen to him if he had to ride to the Carswells and admit failure, admit to them that Clint Winslowe was still alive, hiding out somewhere in the brush along the mountain trail.

Only he doesn't know just how close, thought Clint inwardly. His hands tightened on the butts of the Colts. Very slowly and deliberately, he brought them up until his fingers wcre bar-straight on the triggers, the barrels resting on the top of the smooth slab of rock. There was an open space, perhaps thirty yards in length across which the men would have to ride to come up to the place where Wingate and

Clint lay in waiting. By now, Clint's eyes had become accustomed to the pitch blackness and he could make out the individual riders quite clearly as they spurred their tired, jaded mounts forward. Once, he heard Varges call something to the men behind him, but it was impossible to make out the words and he could only guess that he was ordering the men to move up. Already, they were strung out in a loose, ragged line as their horses struggled down the slope.

'Give 'em another few yards,' whispered Wingate harshly, in an exhalation of breath. 'We don't want to give those at the rear too much warning, or they'll get under cover so fast we won't be able to shoot 'em down.'

There was sense in that, reasoned Clint tightly. He felt his fingers jerk a little as they rested on the triggers of the six-guns. He did not realize that he had been holding his breath for the past minute and that it was now hurting in his lungs. He let it go slowly, tensed himself behind the rock.

A minute passed, then he sensed, rather than felt, the man beside him stiffen abruptly and knew that the time had come. The guns jerked against his wrists as he squeezed the triggers. The man riding immediately behind the sheriff toppled from his horse and pitched to the floor of the trail without a murmur. Varges jerked himself savagely to one side. His horse reared viciously, pawing at the air with its forelegs as the shots rang out and the echoes chased themselves along the walls of the trail.

With an oath, Varges flung himself down out of the saddle, hit the ground and rolled several feet before moving out of sight behind one of the rocks. It was impossible to tell whether he had been hit or had merely fallen awkwardly. The sound of gunfire filled the still air as Clint fired again and again. The men in the posse had been caught on the wrong foot. Half-asleep, they had never stood a chance. Three more fell out of the saddle with wild cries as the bullets slammed into them. Frightened horses reared and lunged as their riders fought to control them. One man failed utterly and the frightened animal, lashing furiously, raced down the trail, then plunged off it to one side, where the canyon wall fell sheer for fifty feet or more. Out of the corner of his eye, Clint saw horse and rider teeter for a moment on the edge of the canyon, then topple sideways. There was a wild yell from the man followed a split second later by a shrill scream from the horse as they plummeted down the canyon face into the narrow valley below.

Lying behind the rock, Clint could hear the bullets striking above him, whining off into the night in murderous ricochet, as the volley of return fire cut through the air around them. Varges was still alive, of that much Clint was certain. He could hear the sheriff yelling orders to those of his men still on their feet.

He guessed there were four or five men at least, still alive and ready to use their guns. Some of them had crawled off the trail and a moment later, the firing swung round as they worked themselves into fresh positions, pouring lead in from a different direction. Clint guessed at their intentions. They meant to swing round, box them in, hoping to cut them down from all sides. Whatever happened, they couldn't be allowed to work their way behind them.

As he lay there, every muscle in him was so tight that his whole body began to ache intolerably. He glanced out of the cover of the rock, across the trail and saw the dark shape that slid smoothly from one side to the other, moving from cover to concealing cover. He fired instinctively, saw the man leap forward as if pushed in the back. Before the other could recover his balance, Clint fired again, heard the man die with a grunt and sigh. His mind was very clear, very sharp and he seemed to hear every single sound with a kind of magnified importance. Beside him, firing with his left hand, Wingate sent shot after shot into the darkness, forcing the posse to keep their heads well down out of sight.

'They're trying to work their way behind us,' Clint snapped in a harsh breath. 'We've got to stop that.'

The shooting boiled up once more as the men facing them began firing savage and furious at them. Bullets chirruped among the rocks. Behind them, Clint heard their horses shying at the sound, champing the bits, feet kicking on the hard ground. That made Clint think of the trail in front and behind them very carefully so that he seemed to see every twist and turn in his mind's eye. The main weight of fire shifted slowly, away from the trail and to one side, among the rocks.

Then, for a moment, it died away as if someone had given a hidden signal, and the sheriff's voice yelled: 'Throw out your guns and come out with your hands raised. This is the only warning I'm going to give you. You can't hope to get away, I've got men all around you.'

That was a lie, thought Clint tightly. Varges didn't have enough men left in the posse to surround them, though he could still make things hot for them. Evidently the other knew this and merely wanted them to answer, to give themselves away. Without answering, he lifted his guns and fired in the direction of the other's voice. He heard one bullet strike unyielding rock and go screaming off into the distance.

Return fire was immediate and he had to pull down his head quickly as lead snapped against the flat top of the rock. Deliberately, he weighed up their chances if they stopped there and found them slender indeed, in spite of the number of men they had killed or wounded. He turned his head sharply to look at Wingate, but in that instant, the other suddenly jerked to one side as a bullet smashed into him. For a moment, he remained upright, then he slid slowly down the side of the rock.

Clint threw several shots into the darkness, then bent over the other. The man was breathing heavily and harshly and the front of his shirt felt warm and sticky. Drawing in his breath, he pulled the other's shirt outward from the flesh, tried desperately to see in the faint light. Wingate was still alive, but how badly had he been hit?

'Where did they get you?' he asked hoarsely, bending so that his lips were close to the other's ear, not daring to raise his voice for fear of being overheard. 'Are you badly hurt?'

'In the shoulder,' grunted the other in jerky gasps. 'Damned careless of me. I ought to have watched what I was doing. I never thought that one of them was so close. He must have been less than ten yards away. Where in God's name are they now?'

Cautiously, Clint lifted his head, an inch at a time, until his eyes were on a level with the top of the rock. There seemed to be a growing brightness in the east and the tops of the trees were standing out a little more clearly than before against the sky. Narrowing his eyes, he searched the rocks and boulders for any sign of the posse At first, he could see nothing and there was silence over everything, broken only by the harsh, uneven breathing of the man lying on the ground beside him a few feet away. Then he caught the sudden flicker of movement, a mere shadow that ran from behind one of the boulders and tried to make it across the trail. He fired instinctively, missed, and by the time he brought his gun to bear again, the man had vanished into the dark shadows on the far side of the winding trail.

Cursing softly under his breath, he bent over Wingate again and tried to see where the bullet had entered his shoulder. He finally located the wound, high up, above the shattered right arm. The blood was welling slowly from the wound, running down the pale skin which seemed to glow eerily in the darkness with the black-red stain of blood standing out clearly against it.

Quickly, he plugged it with his bandana rolled up into a tight wad, then tore a long strip from the other's shirt and bound it up as best he could in the circumstances. 'There,' he said finally, jerking the single word out. 'That will have to hold it until I can get you to a doctor. Think you could ride all the way down into Chandler City, if we manage to get past those *hombres* out there?'

'I can try,' grunted the other throatily. 'Besides, it's going to take a hell of a lot more than this to kill me. I've got to stay alive to see the last of the Carswells die and no crooked sheriff and his posse are going to stop me.'

'That's the way to talk,' said Clint, forcing evenness into his voice. He helped the other to his feet, holding him so that he did not lift his head above the rocks and thus risk another bullet. 'Try to work your way back to the horses and get into the saddle. Be ready to ride out once I come back. Once we start riding, nobody is going to stop us. Understand?'

The other nodded his head slowly, gritting his teeth as a spasm of pain cut through his body. 'Don't you worry none about me, Clint. I'll make it all right. How many do you reckon there are still left alive out there?'

'Can't be more than three or four at the most,' replied the other tersely. 'I guess that Varges is still there. Heard him shouting orders a couple of minutes ago. They've left their horses in the trees about thirty yards along the trail. It's getting lighter every minute so if we're to stand any chance at all of getting through them and away, we'll have to move fast and soon.'

The other nodded, then crawled slowly and jerkily through the boulders, cutting back along the trail towards the tethered horses. Clint lay back against the smooth surface of the rock, feeling the coldness of the stone seeping into his flesh through his shirt. With Wingate wounded like that, things would be doubly difficult. Once he got him to a doctor, he would be on his own again. It was pretty clear that the other could not fight in his present condition. It was fortunate that it had been the arm, the hand of which had been smashed by Chet Carswell, that had been hit.

A couple of shadows broke cover and ran forward, flopping on to their stomachs before Clint could bring his guns to bear on them. He cursed himself for thinking about Wingate and not keeping his attention on the men in front of him. That was where the main danger lay. Evidently the others were now trying to rush him. Whether or not they were aware that Wingate had been hit, he did not know. But they must have realized that the longer they waited, the more chance he had of picking them off one by one.

He listened hard and heard nothing. The men out of sight, remained where they had thrown themselves, waiting for him to make the next move. He sucked in a deep breath, feeling the silence crowd around him, the urgent need to make a decision strong within him.

Very slowly, he edged his way back to the horses. Somehow, although the effort it had cost him must have been great in time and pain, Wingate had managed to get up on his horse and now sat, swaying a little in the saddle. He stared down at Clint, his face a white blur in the dim light. His voice was little more than a husky whisper as he asked: 'Where are they now, Clint? Getting ready to rush us, I'll wager.'

'They're out there somewhere along the trail. But so long as they don't know what we intend to do, we'll be all right. Sure that you can hold on to that horse when we start moving? We'll have to ride hell for leather to get through them without getting shot ourselves. I'll let them have a few shots as we ride through. That ought to keep their heads down until we ride clear.'

'Stop worrying about me, Clint,' muttered the other thickly. 'It'll take a lot more than this to put me out of action.'

'Fair enough,' Clint nodded, swung himself up into the saddle, paused for a moment, with his hands on the pommel, then gave a sharp yell, kneeing the horse forward. It responded instantly, jerking along the trail, hoofs sparking from the rocks underfoot. Behind him, Wingate gave a similar yell. Clint heard men's voices raised on either side of the trail as they thundered forward. He thought he heard the sheriff yell harshly, saw a man rise up almost directly in front of him. The horse leapt forward and the man dived to one side to escape the skull-crushing hoofs that pounded within a foot of his head. A few ragged shots came after them, but none of them were close and they were along the trail, cutting around a sharp bend, then climbing sharply before the posse had picked themselves up and were scattering for their horses.

The fact that they had left them several yards away was a point in Clint's favour and it meant that there would be a delay before the posse, those who were still on their feet and able to ride, could reach their mounts and continue the pursuit. It would only be a matter of a few seconds, but with Wingate wounded, every second was precious now.

Turning off the trail a mile further on, they took a twisting downward path, the hoofs of their horses slipping as they fought to keep their balance on the treacherous ground. It slowed their progress to almost a crawl, but it meant that the posse would have some difficulty in following their trail, for it was still quite dark and their visibility was limited to twenty yards or so in any direction.

Five minutes later, Clint heard the sound of their pursuit coming steadily behind them, sounding above the muffled beat of their own horses and with a wounded companion, he knew that it would not be long before that lead was decreased to the point where the men behind them could begin shooting. As he rode, he kept glancing at Wingate out of the corner of his eye. The other's face now held a queer, pasty look and his lips were skinned back from his teeth as he lay forward across the pommel, his left hand gripping the reins as tightly as the pain in his other shoulder would allow him. He wanted to ask the other if he felt sure he could make it, or whether they ought to find some place where they could form a defensive position and tackle the small group of men who still clung to their trail, even though the path wound and twisted down the face of the hills, but he knew that this was not the time for conversation and also that there was little cover here now that they were approaching the open grassland which bordered the chain of mountains.

He knew none of this land. All of it was new and unfamiliar to him, but he was not afraid of losing his way. All his life, from boyhood on, had been spent in country such as this, a blending pattern of wide, open prairie and tall, rugged hills which rose to a blue skyline. With the sun just getting ready to show itself on the eastern horizon, he knew that it would be the simplest thing in the world to hold his direction.

For a moment, there was a sharp, ringing echo scattering broken pieces of sound off the hills and canyons. He lifted himself slightly in the saddle and listened for a repetition of the sound, but it did not come. That single shot had probably been from a high-powered rifle and right now, they were out of range of even that weapon. Wingate had picked out the sound too, for he suddenly raised his head a little, stared round at Clint. The red stain, showing clearly on his shirt in the growing light, looked ugly and out of place.

'They're closing on us fast,' he said, jerking the words out through tightened lips. 'We'll never make it as far as Chandler City. Even if we do, there ain't nothing to prevent those *hombres* from riding in after us.'

'What do you suggest we do then?' Clint called back, raising his voice as the wind that keened around them, threatened to pluck the words from his lips.

'Better head for the Donovan spread. Reckon we ought to have decided to head for there in the first place.'

'That far from here?'

The other shook his head with an effort. For a moment, he almost lost his hold on the reins and his body slipped helplessly sideways in the saddle. Then, with a sudden surge of superhuman strength, he straightened up, waved away

Clint's offer of help. 'About a couple of miles in that direction.' He pointed to their right, across the stretching prairie which reached out in front of them, at the bottom of the slope, going away to the far horizon.

'Then let's go,' gritted Clint. He dug the rowels of the spurs into the flanks of his tiring mount, felt it surge forward for a little while, then drop back into its original pace. He paused at that, knowing that it was better not to try to force the pace beyond the endurance of his mount, even at this stage. There was one consolation. If Sheriff Varges and his men had been out hunting for him all night and possibly all the previous day, then their horses were even more tired than his and Wingate's.

The tall, red-barked trees which bordered the trail at the bottom of the hills, ran before them for a little way, then petered out as they came out on to the level prairie. By degrees, the territory became more open, the horses somehow managed to lengthen their stride and they began to put plenty of distance between the hills and themselves. But the constant twisting and turning of that hill path had opened Wingate's wound again and the blood was oozing into his shirt. Soon, they would have to slow their pace or the other would be dead before they reached the Donovan ranch.

The sun popped up over the eastern horizon, flooding everything with a brilliant red glow. Soon, he told himself, the heat would come and it would grow, adding its discomfort to the pain in the other's body. There was a definite limit to what a man could be expected to take, even a man so consumed with hate that he seemed to have an inexhaustible reservoir of energy and strength.

Throwing a swift glance over his shoulder, he saw the riders coming down off the mountain trail, out on to the prairie. They had somehow taken a pathway which had carried them slightly parallel to their own and now they were cutting into the open country a little to their left and nearer than he had thought.

They were riding diagonally now, trying to head them off, almost as if Sheriff Varges had divined their intention, knew that they had decided against heading for Chandler City and were instead, moving towards the Donovan ranch.

There were only four of them now, out of the original posse. Some he had seen turn back for Dodge and he guessed that the others were lying up there in the hills, either dead or badly wounded. But even four would be enough with Wingate in no fit condition to handle a gun and he himself was short on bullets. He tried to visualise the distance separating them, but with the sunlight shining full in his eyes, it was difficult to make a proper estimate. He dug spurs again, ignoring the sudden rearing of his horse. Behind them and to one side, another shot blasted but fell short. They were still out of range, even for the rifles.

'How much further?' he yelled at the top of his voice.

'Too far, I reckon.' He could only just hear the other's words. 'They're pulling up on us so fast we'll never make it. You ride on alone. I'll drop behind and keep 'em occupied until you get clear. Tell Donovan what happened. He'll know exactly what to do.'

For a moment Clint deliberated the proposition within himself. Inwardly, he knew that logically, this was the only thing to do, the only real chance they had of stopping the Carswells from robbing that stage if they still intended to go through with their plans. But a little voice in his conscience continued to prick him and he knew that, whatever happened, he could not leave Wingate to these men, for after all it had been the other who had saved his life up there in the hills.

'Nothing doing,' he called back. 'Think you can stick it in the saddle?'

'I'll try,' grated the other. His face was twisted now into a mask of pain. 'But it's your only chance to go on alone and let me hold 'em off. I've still got a score to settle with Varges myself.'

'You've got a bigger score to settle with Chet Carswell,' Clint told him. 'Just keep holding on to those reins. We'll make it. They can't touch us even with the rifles yet and their aim won't be too good trying to pick us off with rifles while still in the saddle.'

That much was true, he told himself fiercely, but only just. It was only a matter of minutes before the posse came within shooting range of them and he knew they could not coax another burst of speed from their mounts. They were already giving everything they had and it just wasn't enough. Those men behind them must have rested up during the day and possibly the earlier part of the night. Their mounts seemed to be fairly fresh even now.

Wingate called: 'This way.' He pulled around his horse's head with a sudden effort that brought the sweat popping out on to his forehead, and pointed with his good hand. Clint glanced up, slitting his eyes against the glaring disc of the sun, still lying close to the horizon. In front of them was a low, gently-lifting rise. A small cluster of trees stood on the crest of it and just beyond, he noticed the boundary fence which indicated the perimeter of the Donovan ranch. He urged his horse towards it. They had to get through that fence if they were to stand any chance at all, but knowing Varges, he would dare even Donovan's wrath to get at them, even to the point of riding on to the other's spread after them. They would still be quite a way from the ranch-house and any help.

A bullet screamed over Clint's back a few seconds later as more firing broke out behind them. The posse was closing in on them fast, urged on by Varges. Moments later, they reached the boundary fence, working their way along it as Wingate sought for the gap through which they could pass. To have set their tired horses at the fence itself, would have been asking for trouble. But all this was costing them precious seconds. He could hear the angry shouts of the men behind them as they came crowding forward close on their heels. Bullets spattered over their heads and buried themselves with leaden thuds in the trunks of the trees. Then Wingate gave a sudden shout, turned his horse sharply to one side. Clint followed him closely, saw the narrow gap in the wire and passed through. Now there was no time to be lost. Swiftly, he urged his mount up the grassy slope. At the top, where they were exposed to the fire from below, clearly outlined against the skyline, he kept his body low over the horse's back, head well down as more shots rang out.

The sheriff's voice, harsh and triumphant, rang out behind them: 'Better halt right there, Winslowe and you too, Wingate. Throw down your guns and lift your hands high, or we'll shoot.'

'Go to hell,' yelled Wingate weakly. He kicked his horse with the spurs. For a moment, horse and rider stood out against the sunlight. Then he was gone, over the brow of the rise, down to the other side. Clint ignored Varge's call and continued after the other. His horse was a surefooted brute. Had it missed its footing on the dew-covered grass of that slope, everything could have been lost. Something plucked at his sleeve as he rode after Wingate and another bullet scorched its way along his arm like the sting of an insect.

'Follow them through.' Clint heard Varges shout the sudden order. 'Those men are outlaws, men wanted by the law. We have every right to ride on to this spread after them.'

Evidently the men with him were not so sure as he was that Donovan would allow them to go riding over his spread in this fashion, or that he would turn these men over to them if they did manage to reach the ranch.

He sucked in a deep breath, felt the wind in his face as his horse thundered off the rise and struck out across the range. He had covered less than twenty yards before he realized that Wingate had reined his mount and that there was a large group of men a little distance away, already moving slowly in their direction. He recognized the man in the lead immediately, even though he had only caught fragmentary glimpses of him in the darkness in Chandler City. So this was Donovan, the man who owned the largest spread in the territory.

He drew rein beside Wingate, reaching out and helping the other from the saddle as he swayed weakly. Behind him, the four men came riding up and he heard Varges shout in a tight, authoritative voice: 'All right, Winslowe, just throw down your gun and no tricks mind or we'll shoot to kill this time.'

Clint turned slowly in the saddle and stared across at the other. 'If you want my gun, Sheriff,' he said, deliberately stressing the final word, 'then I suggest that you come and get it yourself.'

The other paused and an ugly look spread rapidly over his thin, pinched features. The watery blue eyes held a killing look. Then he relaxed momentarily and turned to face Donovan as the other came riding up, his men behind him.

'Sorry we had to ride through your fence, Mister Donovan,' said Varges softly, 'but we've been hunting these two men down for a couple of days. Where that one came from, I'm not sure.' He pointed the barrel of his gun in Wingate's direction, 'but the other is Clint Winslowe. He was tried and convicted of murder in Dodge a couple of days ago. Unfortunately, he managed to bust himself out of jail and headed into the hills. That's where he must have met up with this man who tried to help him escape. I want 'em both now.'

'I see.' Donovan turned piercing blue eyes on Clint. 'You got anything to say to these charges before I turn you over to Sheriff Varges, cowboy?'

'Only that they're all trumped up just to get me out of

97

the way,' said Clint curtly. 'He reckons that I shot a couple of honest citizens of Dodge down in cold blood.'

'And did you?' There was no expression in the older man's tone and his eyes still held Clint's gaze.

'I shot them down in fair fight. They tried to bushwhack me in the street. And they were not honest citizens as he tried to make out. They were Bart and Brad Carswell, both outlaws and with a price on their heads. But I reckon that Wingate here knows a little more about that than I do. He seems to know why those two outlaws were in Dodge – and if what he says is true, then it means that the sheriff here is tied in with the outlaws. Reckon it might help if we got one of the Rangers in on this.'

'We would all expect you to lie your way out of this if you could,' said Varges with a thin sneer. He turned to Donovan. 'This man had a fair trial and he was found guilty of murder by the jury. There are plenty of witnesses in Dodge who testi-fied that he shot down both of those men. And as for them being the Carswell brothers, that's ridiculous and he knows it. They wouldn't dare show their faces in Dodge.'

Clint opened his mouth to make an answer, but before he could speak, Wingate lifted himself upright and faced the sheriff. 'You're a goddamned liar, Varges. I've been doing a little scouting around myself these past few days. And I found out one or two things which I reckon ought to be brought out into the open. Those witnesses of yours were all paid to testify in the way they did. As for this witness who failed to turn up at the trial to clear Clint's name, I have an idea who she might have been and I might even know why she never turned up.'

Varges shrugged. He still kept his gun trained on Clint's chest. 'You're coming along with me,' he said thinly. 'That warrant for your arrest is still in force in Dodge and there's a rope waiting for you the minute you get back. You won't burst out of jail again, I promise you.'

Clint wondered whether he might risk a move for his

gun. At least, he told himself savagely, he could take the sheriff with him; and that would mean there would be one polecat less for the others to take care of. Then he relaxed as Donovan said tautly: 'Reckon they've got a point there, Sheriff. Could be you were mistaken about that shooting incident. Better not act too hasty when there's a man's life at stake.'

'Now see here, Mister Donovan,' said the other harshly, a little blusteringly as he twisted in his saddle. 'I represent the law in Dodge and this man has been declared guilty of murder. He's got to hang and I intend to see to it that he does.' For a moment, his gaze clashed with Donovan's, but it was the sheriff who looked away first. There was a faintly angry, stubborn look on the rancher's bluff features. He said softly: 'You ain't in Dodge right now, Sheriff. You're on my spread, I represent the law here and I say that these two men stay with me until I've had a chance to satisfy myself about their guilt. If they are as guilty as you say they are, then they'll still be here for you.'

'You're making a big mistake, Donovan,' said Varges angrily. For a moment, the hand holding the gun lifted a little, started to swing in Donovan's direction, then paused as he found himself staring down the muzzles of half a dozen Colts.

'No,' Donovan shook his head slowly. 'I reckon you're the one who's making the mistake. Better turn your horses and ride back into Dodge before I give my boys the order to run you off my spread. As I said, these men will stay with me until I'm satisfied about their guilt. And if you've got some idea in your mind of gathering a posse and riding out here to take them back by force, I'd advise you to forget it. I've got more men here than you can raise to come and fight me. Remember, whenever I feel like it, I'm going to take Chandler City apart at the seams and if I can do that, I can deal with any posse you bring along. Besides, I have my spies in Dodge too. I'll know every move you make.'

For a moment, Clint had the impression that Varges intended to make a showdown of it at that moment, in spite of the overwhelming superiority of the man who faced him. Then he shrugged, pouched his gun, pulled hard on the reins and swung his horse around. Over his shoulder, he said tightly: 'Like I just said, Donovan, you're going to regret this. Those two men are cold-blooded killers. The folk in Dodge ain't going to like this high-handed method of yours of hiding escaped killers.'

Donovan tightened his lips momentarily into a hard, straight line. 'We'll see about that, Varges,' he said solemnly. 'Now ride before my men lose their patience '

Clint sat in the saddle and watched the sheriff and the other three men ride off, back over the low rise and through the gap in the boundary fence. The thunder of their horses died away into the distance. When he finally stirred and turned back, he saw Donovan's gaze fastened speculatively on him and there was a curious twist to the other's lips.

Donovan said softly: 'Reckon that you have a mite of explainin' to do, mister, if you're to convince me that I was right in taking you out of their hands. I don't usually misjudge men, even at first sight, but I may be wrong in your case. If I am, I'm going to turn you back to the sheriff and I've no doubt that he'll carry out his threat of hanging you as soon as he gets you back into Dodge. On the other hand, if your friend is right, then we may have work to do.'

CHAPTER FIVE

DEATH AT NIGHT

'Guess we'd better ride back to the ranch now that little bit of trouble has been straightened out,' suggested Donovan quietly. 'There's a lot of talking we have to do and it looks as if your friend needs to get that bullet out of his shoulder. I'll get one of my boys to ride into Chandler City and fetch Doc Sweeney.'

Clint nodded, urged his horse forward as two of the riders helped Wingate to mount up into the saddle. He seemed to be in a bad way now, his face grey, his eyes sunk deep into his head with dark circles under them. It was as if that last effort of standing up to Sheriff Varges had proved almost too much for him, taking the last of his strength from his body. Once he was safely in the saddle with a mounted man on either side of him, one taking the reins to lead the horse forward, they set off through the rich pastures which grew at this end of the long, fertile valley. Clint rode beside Donovan, studying the other closely, interestedly.

This was the first time he had an opportunity to see the man clearly. Black-bearded, with flashing blue eyes, he commanded a magnificent figure as he sat tall and straight in the saddle, head held high and by not much of a stretch of the imagination, Clint could visualise him in Confederate uniform, leading his men against the invading soldiers of the North in the Civil War between the states not too many years before. Now, he seemed to have settled down but still, in spite of that, he seemed to be fighting his own private war against the cardsharps and rustlers in Chandler City and the surrounding territory and judging from the way he had handled Varges, he was a man used to giving orders and expecting to have them obeyed promptly and without question – a man to have as a friend, but a bad and dangerous enemy.

Half an hour later, riding at a slow pace because of the wounded man, they topped a low rise and Clint caught his first glimpse of the Donovan ranch, spread out in front of them. As he had half suspected, it was laid out in the manner of the prosperous plantations of the Deep South with a wide porch which faced south, catching all of the warmth of the summer sun. There were two corrals on either side of the main cluster of buildings and half a dozen barns with the stables to the north. A magnificent place, thought Clint to himself with a faint touch of nostalgia rising within him. Small wonder that there were many men in the territory who were deeply envious of this man and would give anything to bring him to his knees. Evidently, his vast herd would be the prey of every rustler and cattle-thief in the area. There was no doubt that Donovan would have need of every gunman he hired to protect his spread for only a strong and determined man with a private army of trustworthy men could hope to survive in this territory for long.

Dismounting in front of the long porch, Clint waited while Wingate was helped from his horse and carried through into the house. Then he fell into step beside Donovan as the other motioned him forward.

'You can bunk with the boys tonight and shift your gear into the bunkhouse later,' he said. 'But right now, I'd like to have a little talk with you, get to the bottom of this business, because I have a strong suspicion that it could concern me. There's breakfast ready in the house if you'd care to join me. I don't reckon you've had a decent meal for some time.'

Clint nodded in agreement. Now that the immediate danger was past and there was time for reflection, he realized how tired and hungry he really was. He also had the feeling that if Doc Sweeney arrived soon and knowing Donovan, the doc would come a-running as soon as he got the message – Wingate stood a good chance of pulling through in spite of the blood he had lost and the rough treatment that he had undoubtedly received during their flight from the posse.

It was cool inside the ranch, a pleasant change from the blazing heat of the sun now well above the eastern horizon and Clint sank gratefully into the chair which the other indicated, feeling the weariness which soaked in an enervating wave through his limbs and taut muscles. Donovan gave orders for the breakfast to be brought in, then sat down opposite Clint and studied him speculatively.

'You know, you don't look like one of the ordinary gunslingers we get in these parts,' he said suddenly, 'and as I said before, I usually pride myself on being a damned good judge of character.'

'I didn't start carrying a gun and using it, by choice,' Clint said harshly. 'But some years ago, a gang of outlaws murdered my family. I'm the only one left now and I swore then that I would trail them, hunt them down wherever they tried to hide and kill them all. I'd also make sure that they knew who had killed them so that they could take that knowledge to hell with them.'

'The Carswells?' There was no surprise in Donovan's voice and he made it sound more like a statement of fact than a question.

'That's right. I lost them back in Arkansas, then heard that they might have headed this way looking for richer pickings and running from the law at the same time. Things were getting a little too hot for them back there. I was in Chandler City when I heard from Wingate that they were operating in this area, especially over towards Dodge. So I headed into Dodge but it seems that news of my intentions got there before I did.'

A negro servant brought in the food and coffee, set it out on the table in front of them, then went out noiselessly, a dark shadow of a man who seemed to give the impression of having no real existence, but who fitted in well with these quiet surroundings.

When he had gone, closing the door softly behind him, Donovan motioned to Clint to begin, then leaned back in his chair, placed the tips of his long, tapering fingers together and said: 'Somebody rode into Dodge ahead of you, presumably to warn Varges and indirectly the Carswells that you were on your way.'

'It sure looks like that. Whoever was tipped off, they also tried to kill me before I reached Dodge. Some *hombre* tried to shoot me down with a rifle just before I hit the outskirts of Dodge. He was a poor shot, fortunately for me.'

For a moment, Donovan's eyes hardened, his jaw set into a firm line. Clint felt a twinge of surprise at the sudden change, then he went on evenly: 'That's just the sort of low-down trick I would have expected them to pull, particularly that crooked Sheriff back in Dodge. When they failed at that attempt, they set up this meeting with the Carswell brothers, Varges making doubly sure on his own account that you would face a murder charge, just on the off chance that you came out of that gunfight alive.'

'Then you do believe that I killed both of those outlaws in self-defence?'

'I never really doubted it but my feelings, no matter how strong they may be, won't be enough to clear your name completely. You've got to find this witness you spoke of, get her to talk.'

Clint drained his coffee, sat back, feeling better with

food inside him. 'I've been turning that over in my mind all the way here. At the moment though, it doesn't seem all that important compared with other things. So long as I'm here, I guess I'm safe from Varges and there's something a heap more important to do right now. We've got to find out somehow if that gold shipment has gone through yet on the stage and if it hasn't, we have to stop the Carswells from getting their hands on it.'

'Ah yes, the gold.' Donovan rubbed his chin thoughtfully. 'I figure I can put out a few feelers about that without arousing too much suspicion in certain quarters. But now that you've told me all of this, I'm more convinced than ever that we'll have to go after the Carswells.'

'You mean up into the hills?' Clint snapped him a quick glance as he rolled a smoke. 'But even with all of your boys with you, you'd never find them. That area is honeycombed with pathways and forgotten trails and there are a thousand places where they can be hiding out. Besides, they could spot you coming miles away and lay an ambush for you, shoot you all down before you knew they were there.'

'I've considered that,' muttered the other quietly. His beard jutted out in an even more aggressive manner. 'Can you suggest anything which stands a better chance of success. After all, you've been up into the hills with Wingate. He knows them better than any man I know.' A wry smile twisted the other's features for a moment. 'Possibly because he was an outlaw at one time, until Chet Carswell finished his career in that certain, if ignominious manner.'

'There's one main trail leading over the mountains,' said Clint. 'I gather that it goes right up to Saddlehorn Pass and then down along the western slopes. But leading off it are countless other trails, some made by the old prospectors. I've a feeling that if the Carswells are hiding out up there, they'll have taken over one of the old mine workings. It would make an ideal shelter and they could post look-outs to watch every trail leading up to it.'

'So what are you suggesting?' asked the other tightly.

Clint leaned forward, blowing smoke into the air. 'I reckon that a small bunch of men would stand a far better chance of getting through into the mountains without being spotted.'

Donovan shook his head slowly but decisively. 'It wouldn't work,' he said harshly. 'I'll admit that you might be able to get in to them, but then what? They'd box you in and finish you off quite easily.'

Clint gave him a surprised, open look. 'I wasn't suggesting that we tried to wipe 'em out. But I could scout around, find out where they are, where they have their look-outs posted. Then we could go in with a big rush and finish the job. No sense though, in riding in to wipe them out, with our eyes shut.' He paused, then nodded, 'They're a mite too clever for that.'

Donovan ran a long finger down the side of his nose, then nodded. 'It might be the only solution,' he admitted gravely. 'But you'll have to ride without Wingate. He's going to be in no condition to hit the saddle for another few weeks and we can't afford to wait that long. The stage carrying all that gold will be passing along the trail in the next few days if it goes at all. We have to be ready by then and don't lose sight of the fact that Varges will be busy too in the meantime. He knows that things are reaching boiling point right now. Chet Carswell will know that you're here by tonight. I only wish I knew what he will try to do about it.'

'I imagine he might get together a few men and come riding down, to try to take me back,' said Clint.

'A few men?' said Donovan. He shook his head. 'You know how many men he can get together up there in the hills if he has a mind to? Close on fifty gunslingers with every man in that bunch a hired killer, an outlaw, wanted by marshals and sheriffs in every state from here clear to the Mexican border. For all we know, he's been waiting for just such an excuse to come riding out here, for a showdown.

And if he does, I guess he can count of most of the rustlers out of Chandler City who're just itching for gunplay.'

Clint said nothing. He had half expected that, but he had not realized that the odds were stacked so highly against them. If everyone attacked the Donovan spread at once, there were not sufficient men here to withstand them. He scowled over the cigarette smoke, tracing aimless lines and circles on the top of the table with his forefinger, trying to think things out and knowing that there might be no solution.

Then he said softly: 'I'm ready to ride back into those hills, to see if I can find out anything about these outlaws. Are there any men you could trust to go with me. I wouldn't need more than half a dozen.'

Donovan grinned, got heavily to his feet. 'You'd better rest up today, be ready to ride tomorrow at first light if you still feel like it. Don't forget—' His grin broadened. 'I'm supposed to keep you here virtually as a prisoner. If Sheriff Varges should learn that I've allowed you to go hunting down those outlaws in the hills, and with armed men to back up your play, he might construe that as going against the law.'

'I imagine that he might,' said Clint, with an equally broad grin. He rose to his feet, studying the other with a great deal of care, with a secret liking for this tall, broad-shouldered man. Already, he was convinced that Donovan had always been a man for the straight and narrow road, and that he would never have followed any other. A man who did not like killing, but who faced up to it when it was the only thing to do, the last resort.

A moment later, there was the sound of riders approaching, fast, and turning to glance out of the window, Clint saw the two horsemen ride into the compound, dust spurting from the hoofs of their mounts. He recognized one of them as the man Donovan had sent into town. The other, black-coated, small and grey-haired, he took to be Doc Sweeney.

They had taken Wingate into one of the rooms at the back of the house and a moment later, Sweeney came in and went along the corridor, into the room, closing the door behind him.

Donovan excused himself and followed. Clint stood there for a long moment, feeling helpless and hating the sensation which was curiously alien to him. How long he stood there, he could not estimate. Then the door at the end of the corridor opened and Donovan came out. He was followed by the doctor, the latter rolling down his sleeves.

Doc Sweeney said, looking up at Clint: 'You were with him when he got that slug in the shoulder?'

'That's right. We were up in the hills. Why – he ain't going to die, is he?' The other smiled weakly, shook his head. 'It would take more than that to kill a man of his calibre. He'll pull through all right. At the moment, he's sleeping. Had to give him something to stop him yelling that he wanted to hit the saddle and ride back into the hills. Seems he must hate somebody a hell of a lot.' His glance sharpened a little. 'Don't suppose you'd know who he intends to kill, would you?'

Clint shook his head in answer. 'No idea, Doc. Guess a man like that picks up a host of enemies during his lifetime. Sometimes, he gets on the right end of a gun and then he finds peace inside himself for a little while until the next time.'

'Mebbe so,' agreed the other solemnly. 'Well, I've done everything I can for him at the moment. The only thing now is rest and we'll let nature do her share of the work of healing him. I'll call back in a week's time, Mister Donovan and check on his condition then. But on no account are you to let him be moved, you understand?'

'Sure, I understand perfectly, Doctor,' nodded Donovan. 'Sorry we had to drag you out here in all this heat, but I didn't like the look of him. He'd lost too much blood for my liking.'

The other nodded, but said nothing. Pausing for a moment, he threw Clint another quizzical glance, then turned on his heel and walked towards the door. A few moments later, Clint heard the sound of his horse as he rode off.

The next morning, there were dust devils dancing in the compound of the ranch and little whorls lifting as the eddies of wind caught them and spun them high. The tight heat was beginning to grow over the ranch and the roof was already shimmering even though the sun had been less than half an hour above the horizon. Clint cast a suspicious look at the sky to the west. It held an oddly yellow look, unlike the rich, deep blue which had been there the previous day and the day before that. There was going to be a sudden change in the weather, he told himself, with perhaps a storm blowing up. Here, it was possible to get winds of tremendous force, blowing up for a few hours and scouring everything with the sand they lifted. Or if the rain came instead, it broke down everything under its wind-driven force.

Donovan came out of the ranch and walked over to where he stood contemplating the western horizon. He said slowly: 'I've picked half a dozen of the men I can really trust to go with you. But be careful. The Carswells are no fools. If they spot you, you're as good as dead.'

'We'll be careful,' Clint promised. 'I value my hide as much as any man.'

'I realize that,' said Donovan gravely. 'But don't let that hatred of yours ride you to the point where you forget all caution and act on impulse. That could be the ending of you.'

'Killing them is something that will come – sometime.' Clint felt the mad urge for revenge stir in his mind, but knew that he could keep it under tight control until the right moment came. He wanted Chet Carswell to cringe and squirm and to know who it was that killed him after he begged for life – and why he had to die.

Out of the corner of his eye, he saw the six men who rode into the yard. They sat their horses easily and carried their guns low on their hips. One glance at their hard faces, lips drawn thin, told him that these men would not flinch if it came to a showdown, that he could trust them to stick with him no matter what happened. That was good, he decided. The task he had set himself was not going to be easy, but if they were to defeat these outlaws, then it was something which had to be done.

'Here's your horse,' said Donovan quietly. He nodded his head towards the negro who walked forward with Clint's mount. Swiftly, he climbed up into the saddle, checked his own guns, fingered the belt around his waist, noticing that every pouch was full, then took the reins and jerked the horse's head around.

The other men sat in their saddles, waiting. For a moment, Clint threw a swift glance in the direction of the ranch. Somewhere in there, Wingate lay on a low bed, with his shoulder bandaged up, struggling to keep life in his wiry, broken body. His lips thinned as he turned away. He felt certain that if the other did pull through it would be his hatred which would be the dominant factor in his recovery. Then he touched spurs to his horse and rode out of the compound into the hot, dry sunlight, the rest of the men swinging into line behind him. There was the harsh feel of the sand-filled wind on his face but the burning touch of it faded a little while later as he hit the thick grass of the spread and headed for the boundary fence beyond which the mountains rose tall and harsh against the sky.

They rode in silence, each man engrossed in his own thoughts, but all of their eyes were turning towards the undulating summits of the mountains, watching them spec- ulatively, thinking ahead, wondering what their chances of being alive at that time the next day might be.

As he rode, Clint let his thoughts slip back in time a little way. He still could not stop himself from wondering about that woman. Who was she that she should have passed up the one chance to clear his name and possibly save his skin, for she could not possibly have known that he would get the chance to break out of jail before they strung him up from the nearest convenient tree. He let his thoughts slide slowly through his mind. There had been something strange about her manner, he thought, looking back. She had seemed a woman supremely confident of herself and her interest in him had been a little more than mere curiosity. It was almost, he decided, as if she had known him, had realized why he was there and what he had set out to do. But where was she now? Still in Chandler City or back in Dodge? No matter where she was, it seemed highly probable that she would know that he was free; she might even know that he was working with Donovan in an attempt to clean up this place, to rid it of these outlaws who plagued the territory and made it difficult for decent men and women to live in peace.

For a short moment, his thoughts ran fast and uncertain. It was as if he was outthinking himself, trying to put himself into someone else's position and think as they would. They reached the fence, rode through, lit out across the open prairie. He doubted if the Carswells would have men watching as far out as this. They would keep near their hide-out until they decided to ride down into town and it would be useless to spread out their forces to watch every possible route up into the mountains, when they could use fewer men to watch closer to home.

It was almost noon before they rode into the foothills and began to climb. Here they had to ride in single file and moving up into the lead, Clint kept his eyes on the trail ahead, letting them roam over the territory through which they had to pass, watchful for the first sign of trouble. He had been lucky the other time he had ridden through these hills, along these twisting, winding trails. Then he had had

Wingate with him, a man who knew this place like the back of his own hand, and also on that occasion, the Carswells had not been deliberately looking for him as they were probably doing at that very moment. He didn't doubt the truth in what Donovan had said, when he had claimed that Chet Carswell would know that he was in with Donovan by the previous night. Varges would lose no time in telling him of what had happened, how Donovan had taken him out of their hands. But it was a little difficult to visualize what Carswell would do once he got that information. He would be a desperate man. Without the vital information from his two brothers, now lying under the cold earth on Boot Hill, he would have to make other plans for robbing that stage and it would not be easy. He would not want anybody crowding him now.

Such a man, if pushed too far, might act on impulse and that meant he would be unpredictable. Clint turned that thought over in his mind, then pushed it away. They climbed up to the narrow pathway which ran along the rim of the lower slope, where the ravine fell away from them in a steep rush of rock, down to the floor of the chasm some fifty feet below If any man tried that ride without a sure-footed beast, he would almost certainly fall to his death below, his body a mangled, bloody thing on the needle-sharp rocks which thrust themselves up from the floor of the ravine.

Turning his head once, Clint glanced at the men following him slowly in Indian file. There was a tightness on their faces and he thought he saw the look of fear in their eyes whenever they turned their heads and glanced down into what lay a foot or so to their right. But they continued to follow him, allowing the horses to pick their own pace. To try to force them here could easily mean disaster. Satisfied, he swung his gaze back to the front. The narrowness ended less than twenty yards ahead. Once beyond that point, they moved between tall, rearing boulders which would provide them with plenty of cover as they worked their way higher towards the summit. Clint had already formed an idea in his mind as to where he might find the hide-out of these outlaws. There would be countless mine workings here, but it would have to be one which commanded an excellent view of the whole mountainside, as far as Chet Carswell was concerned. He would not be satisfied with anything less than that, Clint felt certain. That factor, in itself, limited the choice of position to sizeable proportions.

As he rode, he had the odd feeling that they were being watched all the way, but that the eyes which watched them were not particularly unfriendly eyes and there was not the feel of a gun on his back as he had experienced before. But though he turned his head often, his keen gaze probing the rocks and shadows which lay on all sides of them, he saw nothing. There was no sign of any danger. A moment later, his horse reached the wider part of the trail and he moved forward more quickly to make room for the men behind. They edged across carefully, not breathing easily until they had safely navigated that stretch of the trail. Clint felt a stirring of grim amusement as he watched their faces. They might have to pass across it far more quickly on the way back if they should run into trouble. He wondered how many of them would pause to think of the chasm which lay on the very edge of the trail if the Carswells and their gunmen were on their heels.

A little before night fall, the wind sprang up, swirling about them with a growing intensity. It swept down off the tall summits of the mountains, hot and dry, with dust driven hard against them as they rode into it, heads lowered, trying to keep the biting, scouring grains out of their eyes and mouths.

Halfway along the winding trail, with half a mile to go before they hit the first of the thick timber, the full fury of the storm hit them, catching them out in the open. It was difficult to breathe properly and although he tied his bandana around his mouth, motioning to the rest of the men to do likewise, the force of the wind was so great that it pushed the grains of sand right through the thick material until they clogged the back of his throat and blocked his nostrils. His eyes felt as if they had been rubbed with pieces of rough stone and it was difficult to see the trail ahead through the red, painful glare that hovered in front of his vision.

If there were any outlaws on the look out, it was just possible that this terrible wind would keep their heads well down and they would not be as alert as they might have been. Also, the keening of the wind, which at times rose to a shrill shriek in their ears, would muffle the sound of their horses until they were too close for any warning to be given.

They rode into the timber and the sudden easing of pressure against their bodies as they swayed forward in the saddle was so swift that for a moment they were all off balance. Swiftly, Clint righted himself in the saddle, lifted his head and blinked several times to enable him to see in the sudden dimness where the sawing branches of the trees succeeded in blotting out the flooding sunlight. This was where the danger might be, he decided. The old mine workings lay on the far side of the timber line, less than two miles distant. From there, they would stretch almost clear to the summit and continue down the other side of the mountains.

He debated whether to continue riding while it was still daylight or to rest up among the trees until nightfall, knowing that by then the storm might have blown itself out, and with a moon it would be possible to go forward unseen. He waved the men to a halt among the trees, slipped from the saddle and rubbed the side of his cheek where the wind-driven sand and dust had scoured it raw There was a thin smear of blood on his hand when he looked down.

One of the men, a tall, sour-faced man named Grainger came forward. 'You figure on staying here until the storm blows over?' he asked.

'That's right. Bent over the necks of the horses we can't see trouble if it comes. Besides, once it gets dark, if the storm is clear by then and I reckon it will be, there'll be enough moonlight for us to see by and we can lead the horses, wait until we spot something suspicious and then go forward on foot.'

'Oh hell,' said the other tightly. 'If we wait, they may be miles away from here by nightfall.'

'Why do you say that?' Clint asked.

'Ain't it obvious? They know that you're in with Donovan and they must have you sized up as a dangerous man. They won't stay here and wait for you to come to them because they know you can cause a lot of trouble if you take your story to the marshal. So they'll be out riding for you, probably picking up Sheriff Varges and some of his men in Dodge on the way.'

That thought had occurred to Clint and he had dismissed it almost instantly. If Chet Carswell had intended to ride out for him, he would have done so long before this, especially if he had known about it the previous evening. He told this to the other, but Grainger did not seem convinced. Nevertheless, he did not argue further. He had had his say and that was enough for him.

For three hours, the sun moved in a sullen red glow down the sky towards the west, touching the tops of the mountains and vanishing beyond them leaving the world still in daylight. The wind slowly abated and the branches of the trees no longer whipped so violently over their heads. Once, during that long period of waiting, when every minute seemed an endless eternity, Clint thought he heard the drumming of horses in the distance, but the sound although it persisted for some time, never seemed to come any closer and he finally ignored it and settled down with his back against the trunk of one of the trees, his hat tipped forward over his face, to shield it from the wind which occasionally managed to find its way through the trees.

Not until an hour after sunset did the storm finally blow itself out over the rangeland below them. The stars came out in a clear sky, which seemed to have been polished by that scouring dust, and winked at them brilliantly between the branches. The moon rose fifteen minutes later, huge and almost full, giving plenty of light to see by.

Mounting up, they rode to the edge of the timber, then slid from the saddles and led their horses forward along the rocky trail, through open country where danger could lurk at every turn.

They moved along short, switchback courses, higher and higher along the edge of the cliff until finally, they came to the first of the old mine workings. While five of the men waited on the edge of the area, Clint and Grainger went forward, noiselessly, flitting like shadows from one tumbled-down shack to the next, ears and eyes alert for the faintest sound and the slightest movement. But the entire place was deserted and they moved on to the next a quarter of a mile or so distant. The hills were full of shadows now and the silence pressed down on them, thick and oppressive.

Then, abruptly, something moved almost directly ahead of him. Instantly, Clint stiffened into immobility, realizing in that same moment that Grainger had either seen the movement too, or had followed his lead, knowing that something was wrong, for he went down on one knee too, staring into the darkness ahead.

After a moment, Clint edged his way back to him. 'Something moved up yonder among those rocks,' he whispered softly. 'Could have been a man on watch. I don't see anything now.'

In reply, the other handed his gun to Clint, then pulled a long-bladed knife from its sheath. 'This will make no noise,' he promised. 'I thought I saw him too. He must be suspicious.'

Be careful,' Clint said. He knew that by right, he ought to be the one to go forward to deal with this man, but he knew that the other had probably used that knife before on similar occasions. It was an old Indian method, quick and noiseless. In the circumstances, that was what they needed. A single gunshot could rouse a whole hornet's nest, bringing the outlaws down on their necks. He watched with tightened breath as the other slithered away into the rocks which bordered the trail at that point. The position where he had seen that sudden movement was some twenty yards ahead of where he now lay, crouched behind the boulders. He strained his eyes in an attempt to pick it out again, but without success. Grainger was a good man and he had full confidence in him. Donovan evidently trusted him implicitly and that ought to be good enough for him. But there seemed little doubt that the look-out he had spotted at the edge of his vision, must be alert and watchful. Everything depended on Grainger getting behind him with that knife without being seen or heard. If he failed, they might just as well have used a gun.

He could sense the seconds grinding past as he waited there. One by one, the other men crept up to him, keeping their heads low, seeming to guess at what had happened without the need for him to explain. As his eyes became more assustomed to the dimness, he could see that the cliff which faced them was composed of rock and earth with small patches of scrub and vegetation dotting it along its whole length and the spot where he had seen the lookout was at a position where the vegetation was densest.

For what seemed an eternity, he lay there with the other men beside him, scarcely daring to breathe. That single slight movement, brief as it had been, was sufficient to tell them that the outlaw camp had to be somewhere close by, and that possibly meant that the rest of the Carswells were there too. He felt the tightness grow within him once more and it was only with a conscious mental effort that he remembered the warning Donovan had given him before be had ridden out that morning, to put all thought of his personal hatred out of his mind on this occasion, otherwise it could lead to danger not only to himself but to the other men with him. What they wanted now, if they could possibly get it, was information, not a lot of dead men.

Then, suddenly, but quietly, he heard the faint sound. It was as if a man had suddenly struck his head against solid rock, uttering a low moan as he did so. Clint waited tensely. For a long moment after that there was neither sound nor movement, then there was the sudden shadow that moved out of the rocks near at land. Clint had his finger already squeezing down on the trigger before he recognized Grainger.

'It was too easy,' whispered the other. He cleaned the blade of the knife on a tuft of grass, then thrust it back into the sheath. 'He was too busy looking in this direction, expecting trouble. Probably he heard our horses and the sound had warned him. He never expected anyone to come on him from behind.'

Clint nodded absently. Shooting a man down with a gun was something he had done often before, something he understood. Then the other man always seemed to have some chance to defend himself. But with a knife, silently and without warning. . . .

He pulled himself together, told himself that the man who had died would have shot them down without any compunction if he had got them in his sights. These men they were dealing with were outlaws, the same brand of men as those killers who had murdered his family. The mere thought helped to stiffen his resolve. How much further it was to the outlaw hide-out he could only guess. He was on the point of waving the men forward when he heard the sound of riders coming along the trail, pushing their mounts at a punishing pace. Swiftly, he stepped back into the rocks, signalled the others to do likewise. The thunder of hoofs came closer, but in the darkness, in the moonlight, and among the rocks which threw back every little echo, it was impossible to judge distance accurately and the riders could have been a mile or only a few hundred yards away.

'Do we take them when they come?' asked Grainger tightly. His voice held an urgent edge and his hand went for his gun.

Clint shook his head. 'We don't know how many there are – or who they are,' he hissed warningly. 'We'll make certain who they are first. If they are the Carswells then we can track them back into the valley. If not, then I'd like to know just who they are and what they're doing out here at this time of the night.'

'You reckon it could be anyone else but the outlaws?' There was a faint note of surprise in the other's tone. He threw a swift, urgent glance along the trail where it wound away in the moolight, dimly seen.

Less than a minute later, the riders, tightly bunched, came into sight. From that distance it was impossible to say who they were, Clint could recognize none of them but as they drew closer, knowing that they would have to pass within a few feet of him, he narrowed his eyes against the moonlight and tried to make out the features of the man who rode in the lead. Not until they were almost on top of them, did he recognize him and he knew then what he had been expecting for so long, ever since he had ridden back into the hills.

The tightly-bunched men rode past their hiding place without a sideways, or backward glance. It would have been the easiest thing in the world to have pulled his gun and shot the leader of that gang of men dead – and there was the knowledge in him that it would have been a good thing if he had done. He had had one of his enemies in his hands and he had let him slip through. But even as his hand had dropped, unbidden, towards his gun, the realization had come to him that this man might be more valuable to them alive, rather than dead.

For the man leading that bunch of men had been Sheriff

Varges, evidently returning from a midnight talk with the Carswell brothers.

CHAPTER SIX

TURN OF THE SCREW

'By all that's holy,' breathed one of the men in surprise, 'that was Varges and some of the men from Dodge.'

'There ain't any doubt where he's been or why,' muttered Grainger. 'That must mean that Chet Carswell and the rest of his bunch of outlaws are in those workings somewhere. Can't be more than a mile away and there ain't many places we'd have to search before we ran them down to earth.' There was a faint note of grudging admiration in his deep voice as he went on: 'Guess you were right all the time about 'em being holed up here. Do we go in after 'em now that their look-out has been taken care of?'

'No.' Clint reached a sudden decision. 'We don't know how many there might be in there and they know this neck of the woods far better than we do. They could slip through our fingers down any one of a dozen tunnels leading right back into the mountains and we'd never smoke 'em out. We're riding after Varges and his crew. We want him alive at all costs.'

'Alive!' The other stood his ground, even as Clint moved forward towards the tethered horses. 'That doesn't make sense. Why Varges? He's just one of the little men in this outfit. He can't help us.'

'Perhaps. But I'm guessing that he knows as much about that stage hold up as anybody, including Chet Carswell. Why else do you figure he's been out here at this time of the night, parleying with the Carswells? Not just to tell them that I'm still alive and with Donovan. Now mount up – and we'll head them off before they hit Dodge.'

The other shrugged resignedly and did not seem too happy about Clint's sudden decision. But Donovan had given orders that they were to follow him and obey him and Clint felt only a momentary twinge of surprise at the other's aquiescence as he finally nodded, turned, and gave the necessary orders to the rest of the men scattered among the rocks.

They rode out fast, hitting leather, following the trail to the south-west for a little way, then swinging right across rough country and through long stretches of thick timber, cutting diagonally towards the trail into Dodge. Varges would not be expecting real trouble, he reasoned, and therefore would not push his tired men and horses hard all the way into town once they hit the main stage trail between Dodge and Chandler City. There was no sign of the other party in the bright flooding moonlight and even the sound of their horses had faded away completely into the distance, but Clint was not worried about that. The trail they were following should bring them well ahead of Varges and his men and give them sufficient time to prepare an ambush on both sides of the trail. He estimated that there had been ten or a dozen men in that bunch which had ridden past them at breakneck speed, but even so, the odds would be in his favour. Those men from Dodge would not fight as well or as fiercely as the men he had with him for few of them would be professional gunmen. They would ride with Varges and even with the Carswell gang provided they got a cut of everything they took and did not have to face up to over-whelming opposition.

They held to the crests of the long, sloping ridges for as long as possible. This meant that in the moonlight, which was now almost as bright as daylight, they could watch the trail down below, pick out anything which moved on it, but they themselves would be backed by the looming bulk of the high mountains and their silhouettes would be extremely difficult to pick out against the mass of dark greys and browns.

An hour's hard riding brought them gradually down the slope, their horses kicking dust and powdered rock under their feet. The main trail now lay less than a quarter of a mile away, clearly visible along a greater part of its length in the bright moonlight and still there was no sign of the men they had been trailing. Reaching the edge of the trail, they reined and Clint ordered the men to spread out, to take cover on either side of the track. The position he had chosen for the ambush commanded an excellent view of the trail in both directions. For perhaps half a mile the wide track stretched away into the moonlight, but closer at hand, ending less than twenty yards away, tall walls of rock lifted sheer on either side and formed a kind of natural channel. He intended to wait until Varges and his men had ridden into this before giving the order to fire.

That way, he figured, there would be little chance of escape for any of them and confusion would panic their horses within moments of the first shots ringing out. He had, however, impressed upon every man with him that no matter how many of the other men were killed in the fighting, he wanted Varges alive and in a fit condition to talk.

He settled his long, lean body into a more comfortable position among the rocks, the cold yellow moonlight flooding over him, touching everything with an eerie glow; a strange, cold radiance that softened the contours of the rocks so that they lost their natural harshness of outline, but which seemed to deepen the shadows which lay in the deep crevasses. He had posted one of the men among a tumbled heap of boulders on top of the long wall of rock which hemmed in the trail. From there, the man would be able to warn them of the approach of the men when they were still more than a mile away.

Absently, he rubbed his chin, pulled his hat down further over his eyes. There was a chill coldness in the air now and he shivered as he pushed himself to his feet, stretching his legs as cramp threatened to twist the muscles into tight knots of agony. They had ridden hard and fast along that winding trail, but it seemed impossible that they could have outridden the others so far. Had he miscalculated some-where along the line? Had Varges been a little too clever for him? A hundred possibilities chased themselves like a herd of stampeding cattle through his mind.

Perhaps things were moving a little more quickly than he had imagined – perhaps Varges had ridden towards Chandler City to pick up more men, ready to help Carswell in any plans he may have had since his brothers had been shot. Certainly, he would have had to do some quick think-ing these past few days if he was still to go ahead with his attempt to rob that stage of the gold bullion. His mind boiled and bubbled within him as he stood there, peering intently along the trail where it stretched empty into the moonlit distance. He shaded his eyes against the brilliant moonlight and watched the man among the rocks, his shoulders just visible above the rounded tops of the boul-ders, waiting tautly for the signal that would tell him and the others that the sheriff and his band had been sighted.

Drawing in a huge breath, he let it go sharply. There was the feeling of defeat and exasperation deep within him and growing stronger and more insistent with every minute that passed. He could guess what Grainger and the others were thinking at that particular moment and he did not blame them if they felt sore at him. Up there, a little over an hour ago, they had had the chance to either shoot down Varges or go in and risk a pitched battle with the outlaws which was what Grainger had wanted to do, knowing that the element of surprise would be in their favour. But he had deliberately thrown away both chances in the hope that Varges would ride this way into Dodge, and they could take him without any real trouble.

Acting on impulse, he went down on to the trail, searched the ground methodically with his fingers for a long moment, then straightened up, hopeful in one respect. There had been no horses heading back into Dodge along that trail for many hours which meant that Varges had not beaten them to this point in the trail. He was just on the point of moving forward when Grainger dropped down beside him.

'Looks like you might have figured wrong, Clint,' he said laconically. 'If they were headed this way we should have spotted them by now unless they stopped somewhere along the trail. Ain't no reason though why they should have.'

Clint tightened his lips into a hard line. 'There ain't no other place they could go except into Chandler City and they've no call to go there unless it's to pick up more gunhawks for Chet Carswell.'

'What makes you so certain that ain't what they've done?' muttered the other. 'They lit out of those old workings in a hurry like they were headed someplace real special.' He paused, glanced up at the moon, running the back of his hand over his mouth. 'If they have done that, we don't stand any chance of overtaking 'em before they reach town. They have too big a head start on us now.'

That was true, thought Clint tightly. But somehow, it didn't figure. A moment later, a sharp urgent yell from the man among the rocks put an end to the chaotic jumble of half-formed thoughts and ideas that had been racing through his mind.

'*Here they come!*'

Clint crossed swiftly into the rocks, crouched down with one of the heavy Colts balanced in his right hand. There was a cloud of dust in the distance, just visible in the moonlight and already his ears had picked out the faint thunder of hoofs on the trail. They were coming forward at a slow gallop, evidently taking their time, unsuspecting. He watched them closely as they came on, his eyes narrowed to mere slits. The tenseness was still there in his body, but he forced himself to relax with a conscious physical effort. When a man had a job like this to do, it was better to do it relaxed rather than all burned up. Half a mile and there was no doubt in his mind that this was the sheriff and his men returning from their talk with the outlaws. His jaw lumped under the skin as he thought of how those decent citizens of Dodge were being fooled all along the line by the crooks who were now running the town. In the olden days, Dodge had been one of the frontier towns which had possessed a straight-shooting, hard-hitting sheriff. Perhaps the people had been deluded into thinking that things were still the same. Little did they know that the law which was supposed to help them was actually being twisted and used against them.

One swift glance told him that all of his men were in position and ready. For a moment, he had a strangely creepy feeling, lying there, knowing that before many more minutes had passed, several of those men riding towards them would be dead, shot down before they even suspected that there was anything wrong. He lay flat, head lifted slightly to see over the flat-topped rock in front of him. The shouts of the men as they talked among themselves could be clearly heard now.

Suddenly there was a different sound as they rode into the trail where the rocks tunneled them in and the echoes of their horses' hoofs were thrown back and reflected many times by the walls of solid rock.

Clint waited for another few moments, the tenseness growing in him in spite of the tight hold he had on himself. Then he lifted his gun, sighted it on one of the men immediately behind the small, slight figure of Sheriff Varges and squeezed the trigger. The gun leapt like a living thing in his hand and the man screamed out loudly in mortal agony as the bullet found its mark. Instantly everything was confusion on the trail as man and beast fought to free themselves from the trap into which they had ridden. He could hear Varges yelling dimly, but the words could not be heard clearly above the shrill neighing of the horses and the stamping thunder of their hoofs. Some of the men with the sheriff began firing blindly into the rocks but it was clear that they did not know where the fire was coming from.

Out of the corner of his eye, Clint saw the man he had posted on the rocks, lift himself so that he was in full view of the men below, losing off shots into the milling riders. Clint crawled forward, keeping his head down, gliding swiftly from one rock to the next, edging all the time towards the edge of the trail. He had to get Varges away from that crowd of men before a stray bullet hit him. With Varges dead, all of this would count for nothing.

A rider burst out of the trail, into the open. Clint swung up his gun to cover him, saw that it was one of the men with Varges and not the sheriff himself. There was an expression of stark fear written all over the other's face as he pulled hard on the reins trying to turn the horse's head, away from the trail and up into the rocks. Clint's bullet caught him in the shoulder and he toppled out of the saddle, crashed down among the rocks and lay still, evidently stunned by the fall.

Forgetting him, Clint rose to his feet and ran forward, leaping over the boulders in his path. A bullet hummed close to his shoulder and he flattened himself against the smooth wall of rock on the edge of the trail. There was the chance that he could get himself shot by one of his own men, he thought inwardly, but his keen gaze had picked out Varges just ahead of him, less than ten yards away and he

127

knew that was a risk he would have to take.

'Sheriff!' He yelled the word at the top of his voice, saw the other turn his head sharply, not recognizing him, probably thinking he was one of the men who had ridden with him. 'Over this way! Quickly!'

The ruse worked. Gigging his horse forward, his face grey with fear, Varges headed towards the side of the trail. He came up to Clint before he recognized him as he stepped back into the moonlight. The hand holding the gun came up swiftly as the realization came to him that he had been tricked, but by that time, it was too late. Reaching out with both hands, Clint caught him tightly around the ankle, and pulled him out of the saddle. Varges fell clumsily, hit the ground with a blow that knocked all of the wind from his lungs. But he still fought desperately, trying to bring up the gun, to line it up on Clint's face and press the trigger.

Savagely, Clint pulled his arm free of the other's encircling grasp, drew it back to shoulder level, then hit the sheriff hard on the point of the chin. His head snapped back under the impact of the blow which had all of Clint's weight behind it. His eyes turned up and glazed as he slumped back. Swiftly, not pausing to look up, Clint hooked his hands beneath the other's arms and dragged him back among the rocks.

Around him, the firing had reached a sudden crescendo. Shots bucketed among the rocks as the riders, caught inside the walls of rock strove to burst out into the open and make good their escape. It was impossible to guess how many had been killed, but their return fire was becoming more accurate as they picked their targets more carefully.

The shouting went on and firing broke out at one point and then another all the way along the rock wall, and each shot that was fired told of more men trapped in the ambush.

Ten minutes later, as the firing slackened a little, four

men, crouched low over the backs of their horses, rode full tilt out of the rocks, cut through the ambush and rode off hell for leather along the trail in the direction of Dodge. A handful of ragged shots followed them into the moonlit darkness, but Clint yelled harshly: 'Let them go. No sense in wasting bullets on them. They won't stop until they hit Dodge and I don't reckon they'll be coming back in a hurry.'

He threw a swift glance at the sheriff, saw that he was still unconscious and then went forward with Grainger into the shadow between the two walls of the rock. They found two men badly hurt, the others were dead, except for Varges and the man Clint had hit in the shoulder and who was still lying face-downward in the boulders.

He straightened up and then looked across at Grainger. 'Varges is back there. He's out cold but there isn't a mark on him. We'll take him back to Donovan's and ask him a few questions.'

'You reckon that he'll talk?' asked the other, as they went back to the horses. 'He's that scared of Carswell that I doubt it.'

'He'll spill everything he knows,' Clint said grimly. 'I can promise you that. I know a few of the Indian tricks myself. Ain't found many folk who could stand up to them for long without yelling.'

Heaving the unconscious form of the sheriff across his saddle, Clint climbed up himself. He sat still in the saddle waiting for the others to mount up, then started out along the trail towards the Donovan spread. At the back of his mind, there was the gnawing possibility that the sound of that gunfight might have carried up into the rocks and Carswell may have wondered about the reason for it.

But there was no further sound of pursuit from the hills and at midnight they reached the perimeter of the Donovan ranch, rode through the outer fence, past the herd of drowsy cattle in that corner of the spread, with the two night herders circling the milling steers, watchful for trouble, never knowing from which direction it might come, with rustlers preying on the cattle at every possible opportunity. On the saddle in front of Clint, Varges suddenly stirred and tried to get up into a sitting position, but Clint pushed him roughly down again with the flat of his hand. For a moment, the other lay there in silence, obviously struggling to recollect himself, to gather his scattered thoughts. Then he twisted his head around, fingered the bleeding gash on the side of his cheek, and squinted up at Clint's impassive face in the moonlight.

For an instant, there was a blank look on his face, no recognition in his eyes, then memory returned. His lips pressed themselves tightly together and he showed a bitter face. 'You don't really expect to get away with this, do you, Winslowe?' he asked throatily. 'Or do you figure that we can't do anything worse than hang you?' He wasn't scared yet, thought Clint, watching the other carefully. Perhaps he must have realized that if Clint had intended killing him out of hand, he would have done so before, when they had been ambushed.

'I'll get away with it,' Clint told him. As he spoke, Grainger edged his horse forward matching its pace with Clint's until he had drawn level with him. He stared down dispassionately at the sheriff, his mouth twisting a little. 'So you finally came around, Varges,' he hissed thinly. 'If I'd had my way back there, you would have been shot down long ago. A double-dealing rat like you doesn't deserve to live. Still, I reckon the folk in Dodge might lay on some special treatment for you once they know that you've been working hand in glove with Chet Carswell and his gang of outlaws.'

'You don't know what you're saying,' mouthed the other. He squirmed for a moment across the saddle, glaring up at Grainger, at the faintly mocking face etched with shadow in the moonlight, but Clint thought that he detected both fear and uncertainty in the other's voice. 'Reckon that you'd better let me go before you really tangle with the law.'

Grainger threw back his head and gave a harsh, mocking laugh which bellowed above the thunder of their horses' hoofs. 'There ain't no law around these parts any more,' he said thickly. 'You saw to that when you threw in your lot with those gunhawks in the hills.'

Varges pressed his lips tightly together and said nothing. He closed his hands into fists, hard-balled, and let them hang loosely down as his body swayed from side to side across the saddle. He had the air of a man who knew he had fallen into the hands of his enemies and that he had to maintain silence at all costs if he wanted to save his own life.

Presently they topped the low rise, came in sight of the ranch and rode down into the courtyard. In spite of the lateness of the hour, there was still a yellow light in one of the windows and a moment later, the door opened and Donovan stepped out on to the porch, staring out into the darkness. 'That you, Winslowe?' he called.

'Yeah.' Clint slid out of the saddle, pulled the sheriff down, forcing him to stand on his feet. 'We got a prisoner with us this time. Maybe we can get him to talk.' He thrust Varges forward, past the side of the corral.

'Who is it? Not one of the Carswells?' Interest quickened Donovan's voice. He stepped forward on to the hard-packed earth of the compound.

Clint shook his head as he prodded the muzzle of his gun into the small of the sheriff's back. 'No,' he said. 'We picked up Sheriff Varges. He'd been out for a night with some of his men, up into the hills. Reckon he was parleying with Chet Carswell and those other outlaws.'

'That's a damned lie.' Varges moved forward swiftly, away from Clint, stepping swiftly over the compound and going up to Donovan, standing in front of the other. 'I was out looking for those outlaws, meaning to take them in. Got word that they might be hiding out in the old 'Lost

Horizon' mine. Took a posse out there with me to try to surprise 'em, then we were ambushed on our way back into Dodge by this killer and some of your hands.'

Clint pouched his gun, strode forward, grasped the sheriff by the shoulder and spun him around savagely. His fist lashed out and although the other guessed what was coming, and tried to sway back out of reach, he was far too slow. Clint's fist hit him hard in the middle of the stomach, sent him staggering back, his mouth jerking open as he gasped for air. His hands, fingers spread wide, pressed themselves tightly over the lower half of his stomach as if to protect him from any more hard swings. Sucking air down into his heaving lungs, he stood there for a long moment, teetering from one foot to the other, head lifted a little, eyes staring up at Clint with a sick intensity, lips peeled back now over his teeth, in a weird parody of a snarl.

'You going to tell the truth now, or do we have to beat it out of you?' gritted Clint. He was aware of the other hands and Donovan watching the proceedings interestedly, but none of them made a move to interfere.

'You can't prove anything,' snarled the sheriff hoarsely. 'And as for you, Donovan—' He straightened up with an effort, pain showing through the mask of anger on his face. 'I'll see to it personally that you're brought to trial with the rest of these men. You're deliberately condoning this attack on me.'

'You were up there in the hills talking with Chet Carswell,' went on Clint slowly as if he had not heard the interruption. 'We saw you and your men riding hell for leather out of the old 'Lost Horizon' mine workings. That wasn't the act of a man who had gone in there to shoot it out with those outlaws.'

Varges turned slowly, drawing himself up to his full height. Hate blazed fiercely out of his eyes. 'We didn't find 'em,' he snarled viciously. 'They either left before we got there or our information was wrong and they weren't within miles of that place.'

Clint opened his mouth to speak, but before he could do so, Grainger had stepped forward, going right up to the other. The faint rustle of the knife as he slid it from its sheath was a soft sound, just audible, but Varges heard it clearly and jerked his gaze down, eyes widening a little.

'This is the knife I used when I killed that look-out among the rocks just outside the 'Lost Horizon' mine where he'd been posted to watch the trail.' He thrust it forward with a swift, savage movement and Varges retreated a couple of paces, almost falling over himself to get out of the way of the blade, until he came up against Donovan and could retreat no further. There was a tightness to Grainger's face which added menace to his tone as he went on: 'If you and your men got past that look-out, it could only have been because you were expected. They probably had him placed there to make certain that you weren't disturbed while you planned the best way to take that bullion stage.'

A flicker showed at the back of the sheriff's eyes but his face betrayed nothing. He kept silent, his gaze fixed on the blue-shining blade of the knife in the other's right hand. Donovan said harshly: 'Guess we'd better take him inside, boys. If he does know anything about this robbery they've been planning, we'll find out before morning.'

As they went inside the ranch, their boots hammering hollowly on the wood of the porch, Donovan turned to Clint and said softly: 'Those men who escaped into Dodge, you figure they might try to get through to Carswell to tell him about the trap you laid?'

Clint shook his head slowly. 'I don't reckon so,' he said deliberately. 'They probably figure that Varges is dead by now and none of them got a good look at us, so they won't know who we are. For all they know, we could have been one of the rival gangs of outlaws from the hills, wanting this gold for ourselves.'

'I hope you're right. There's no difficulty in keeping Varges here, making certain that he doesn't warn Carswell that anything has gone wrong.'

Clint smiled grimly. 'If I know those *hombres*, they'll have hit Dodge in a hurry and they'll stay there, under cover, until this has blown over, not daring to show themselves, just in case Carswell does decide to go looking for them. They aren't the same calibre as the men we're dealing with up in the hills.'

He followed Donovan inside. Varges stood sullenly in one corner of the room, still clutching at his stomach where Clint's bunched fist had thudded into his flesh. The badge on his chest glittered mockingly in the light of the lamp on the table and feeling a sudden surge of uncontrollable anger, Clint walked over, saw the other flinch as if expecting another blow, then plucked off the star, tearing it off the other's shirt. He held it in the palm of his right hand for a moment, staring down at it, mouth twisting, then he threw it on to the table. 'Maybe we'll get a better man than you to wear that someday,' he said thinly. 'You won't be needing it any longer.'

'I'd like to know where you'll be when I come looking for you, Winslowe,' said Varges, between clenched teeth. He sounded tired but not yet beaten. 'If you want to finish, it here and now, let me have my gun back and we'll get it over with.' The colour had gone entirely from his sharp features and his lids drooped over his eyes.

Clint shook his head and smiled frostily. 'You ain't going to get that chance to die quickly and easily,' he said. 'You're going to tell us everything you know about Chet Carswell's plan for holding up that stage. We know that he was relying on his two brothers to get that information for him. Somehow they must have wormed their way into the confidence of the stage company and knew when the real stage would be passing through Dodge on its way into Chandler City and then on east. He had to be sure that he didn't attack the dummy stage carrying nothing but sand in the boxes.'

It had been a shot in the dark, but one look at the Sheriff's face told him that it was true. He went on swiftly, giving the other no time to protest his innocence still further: 'When Bart and Brad died, Chet had to find some-one else to supply him with that information and he had to get the news fast because time was running out. So who better to get it for him than the one man they all trusted in Dodge – Sheriff Varges. The man who had captured those men's killer and brought him to trial. God, how you must have been laughing to yourself that day, Varges.'

'You're just guessing at all this, trying to vindicate your-self,' snapped the other fiercely. He spoke as if trying to convince himself, and there was an odd edge to his voice. 'You've got no proof of this. You're merely groping around in the dark.'

'I don't think so.' Donovan stepped forward. 'I think there's a heap of truth in what Clint says. Now are you going to tell us everything you told Carswell, or do we have to get it out of you the hard way?'

'You don't scare me, Donovan,' said the other thinly, trying to bluster. It was plain to see that he had always considered himself to be tough, ready to face up to any chal-lenge thrown down to him. No doubt, in his fertile imagi-nation, he had visualised himself as the hero in many a gun battle but now he faced up to the real thing and he was no longer sure of himself at all. Clint, eyeing him closely, his fists bunched, saw the man struggle within himself to retain what little spark of manhood he had ever possessed. But it was slipping away from him, fast, draining out of his body like water from a sponge. He seemed to sag, although there was still a look of determination on his face and Clint guessed that there was an even bigger and more demanding fear in his mind, helping to boost up his fading courage; the fear that somehow, by some miracle he could not at the moment imagine, he might get out of this fix with a whole skin and Carswell might carry through his plan and take that stage and everything on it.

If he did, if he carried out the biggest stage robbery in the entire territory, in spite of the odds which were mounting steadily against him, then he might come riding after anyone who had betrayed him and his revenge would be a terrible thing to contemplate.

'Reckon he ain't going to talk without a little persuasion,' said Clint tightly, looking round at Donovan. 'Want me to get it out of him the hard way?'

The other hesitated, threw a swift glance at Varges, then nodded. 'You have to,' he said. 'Much as I dislike that kind of stuff, you must get that information before it's too late for us to do anything about it. Take him into the bunkhouse and work him over.' There was no emotion in the rancher's deep voice. Clint knew that he had accepted the inevitable fact that there was only one way to make Varges talk and tell the truth. He went over to the cringing man, caught him by the arm and pulled him through the door, along the porch, out across the compound and into the long bunkhouse.

Varges gave Clint a strange stare, tried to remain upright as the other hit him hard across the side of the face, drawing more blood from the deep gash on his cheek, snapping his head back.

'Better talk now and save yourself a lot of trouble,' Clint advised him quietly. He looked round him for a moment at the other four men in the bunkhouse, sitting up on their bunks, watching the proceedings. They were more of Donovan's hands and they wouldn't interfere even though they did not know what this was all about. They were the kind who had learned long ago not to interfere in another man's business. They were probably beginning to enjoy what was happening.

Varges knew that he was trapped and like a cornered rat he decided to try to fight. Clint grinned viciously as the other came at him in a low crouch. The man was scared now and slow. He tried to reach out for Clint with outstretched arms, legs shuffling forward, his mouth hanging slackly open as he gulped air down into his lungs. As he came forward, he rubbed at his cheek momentarily, absently, with one sleeve, must have caught sight of the blood on the cloth, for he paused for a second, then whirled savagely. Clint let him come in, then brought up his knee against the other's chest as he bent forward. The crack of his knee hitting the other sounded throughout the long length of the bunkhouse. Varges staggered back, head high, trying to hold himself upright. But he never quite made it. His legs gave way under him and he collapsed on to the floor. Clint did not give him a chance to regain his wind. Stepping forward, he bent, hooked his fingers in the other man's shirt and hauled him to his feet. For an instant, the other swayed against him, half-unconscious, eyes glazed, teeth biting down on each other in pain. Some memory of other fights he had been in must have persisted in his mind, for he still held his body in a half crouch as if to protect himself from any punch in the stomach. But Clint's next blow was to the side of the head. As the other cried out, he jabbed upwards with the toe of his boot in the sheriff's knee-cap. It was not so much a crippling blow as an extremely painful one and the other yelled aloud with the agony of it, as pain lanced along his leg into his body. He fell back against one of the bunks, lay sprawled over it, arms raised to ward off any more blows.

Tight-lipped, Clint moved forward. He felt no compassion for the other. The man was worse than an outlaw. At least they were what they professed to be, but this double-dealing coyote pretended to be the man to uphold the law when in reality he was using it as a shield to cloak his other activities. He drew back his fist to slam in another blow to the face, but Varges had had enough. His manhood and determination had evaporated more quickly than either he or Clint had imagined.

'No, don't,' he said thickly, through smashed lips. 'I'll talk. I'll talk.'

'That's better.' Clint heaved him to his feet, held him there as the other threatened to collapse again. He motioned to two of the other men to come forward and carry the sheriff into the ranch.

Donovan threw a swift glance at the broken figure, then nodded. 'He'll talk now, I guess.'

'He'll tell us everything we want to know,' said Clint meaningly. 'And if he doesn't tell the truth, he'll regret it.'

'I ain't going to shield Carswell,' mumbled Varges throatily. 'He'll probably gun me down when it's all over anyway rather than part with any of that gold.'

'So you've finally got wise to him.' Clint nodded. 'When is that stage due to pass through Dodge on its way to Chandler City and where does Carswell intend to make a try for it?'

'Tomorrow night,' muttered the other without lifting his head. 'The first stage through will be the dummy, packed with armed men to trap him. He knows that though and he'll let it go through. The second stage will be carrying the gold. There won't be too many armed men with it. Just a couple of men riding shotgun and four men inside the coach with the gold. He's going to hold it up right at that spot where you ambushed us tonight.'

Clint nodded. There was the ring of truth to what the other said and that spot he had chosen was just the place that Carswell would have in mind. It had admirable properties which made an ambush almost certain of success.

'How many men will Carswell have with him?' asked Donovan.

'Twenty men of his own and possibly the same number from Chandler City.'

'Forty men, all armed to the teeth.' Donovan nodded slowly. 'We can't match that number unless we can warn the

138

men in the first stage and get them to turn back when he makes his play. That might swing the battle against him.'

'It's our only chance,' agreed Clint quickly. 'In the meantime, I'd like to ride into Chandler City, trying to find what's happening there. They don't know me in that town and I might be able to find out something before tomorrow night.'

Donovan eyed him curiously for a moment. 'That the only reason you want to go there?' he asked solemnly. 'Sure you don't want to try to find this woman who can clear your name in the eyes of the townsfolk of Dodge?'

'If she's there, I'll find her,' Clint promised. 'Though she may be out of the territory by now.'

Donovan nodded. 'Reckon you owe it to yourself to try anyway,' he said, understandingly. 'Better get some sleep before you go. We'll take care of Varges.'

'See that he doesn't manage to slip away otherwise we're all finished,' he said soberly. 'He knows a lot too much now. In fact, I'd say that he's too dangerous to be allowed to live. Later, we might regret not shooting him now.'

Donovan stood silent, thinking of that. The words seemed to have stirred something inside him and he straightened and looked across at the sheriff's bloody features. 'We'll watch him close,' he said harshly. 'If he tries to make a run for it, all of my men will have orders to shoot him down on sight. He won't get off the spread to warn his friends in the hills. I reckon that tomorrow when they try for that stage, they'll get some big surprise.'

Clint nodded as he turned on his heel and walked towards the door. 'If we're lucky, we may get the whole of the Carswell gang. I'm only sorry that Wingate can't be with us when we ride out. He'd have liked to have been there to see Chet Carswell get his.'

'I know.' Donovan nodded, then turned to Grainger and gave orders for Varges to be taken into the room at the back of the house with a couple of men set to watch him every minute.

Going out into the night, Clint sucked down deep gulps of the cool night air. The moon was still as bright as ever and it seemed impossible to believe that so little time had actually passed since they had sheltered in those trees on top of the hill to escape that dust storm and wait for the night before moving on. He walked slowly to the bunkhouse, removed his boots and hung his gunbelt at the corner of the bunk, then stretched himself out m the darkness. A man's voice from the far end of the room said softly: 'Did he talk?'

Clint nodded his head in the darkness, then realized that the other could not see the movement. 'He told everything,' he said softly. He rested back and closed his eyes, trying to shut out his mind, temporarily at least, the thought of what lay ahead of him.

CHAPTER SEVEN

THE TRAP

Clint ate breakfast in the dining room with the ranch crew and Donovan. When he finished, he went out into the corral, roped his horse and was soon in the saddle. Donovan came out on to the porch as he sat ready to move out and threw him a quick glance. 'Be careful, Clint,' he said quietly. 'I wouldn't like anything to happen to you right now, just when we seem to have this thing almost licked. There might be a place for the right man around here when this is all over and those rustlers and outlaws have been smashed for good. Dodge is going to need a new sheriff for one thing and we'll have to make certain that law and order are brought into Chandler City. That town has been lawless long enough. This country has got to grow up if it's to survive the years to come. But I reckon that you know that as well as I do.'

'Sure.' Clint nodded slowly. He could guess how the other felt, just as he had felt himself in those days before his parents had been murdered. But when they had been killed, it was as if something had been burned out of him by the branding iron of hate, and there was a vacuum in his mind that nothing seemed to be able to fill. 'But I don't look on myself as a good sheriff. I've seen too much trouble.'

'Well, anyway, ride on into Chandler City and think things over on the way. But whatever happens, even if you do manage to find this woman you're looking for, you have to be back here by nightfall. We're all depending on you to ride with us against these men. We'll need every man who can handle a gun if we're to succeed against that bunch. And if he manages to bring in those rustlers from Chandler City, we'll have a tough fight on our hands.'

Clint gave a quick nod of his head, then turned his mount and rode out of the courtyard, past the corral and the barns, beside the bunkhouse, out on to the soft grass which stretched away in front of him almost as far as the eye could see. Yes, he thought a trifle wearily, this was good country. A man could settle down here, force his roots into the ground and start up a new life where it might be possible to bury the past, forget the bad things that had happened. But at the moment, that was not possible. They would have to fight and men were going to be killed before that could come to pass.

He rode through the fence, hit the trail and turned left towards Chandler City. The sun struck hot on his back and shoulders and his thoughts ran fast and in an unruly fashion through his mind. For the first time in several hours, he found his thoughts turning back to the girl and in spite of the fact that she had deliberately refrained from coming forward to speak in his defence at the trial in Dodge, there was a warmth in him as the image of her face flashed through his mind. It was odd that anyone should feel that way about a woman they had seen only three times and whose name they did not even know. She had half smiled at him, outside the store just after he had shot those two men and Sheriff Varges was taking him in, but even then there seemed to be a strange reserve inside her, holding her back, as if she could trust neither him or herself. But below that reserve, he had sensed there was a fullness waiting and that fullness had been the hint of a promise.

For a moment, he let his thoughts dwell on her, then he shrugged them away. Time enough to think about that if he managed to find her again, he reflected. But at the moment, he felt certain that she was no longer in the territory, that she had ridden out and was possibly back east now. Certainly, judging from her manner that was where it seemed she belonged.

The journey into Chandler City took him longer than he had expected and it was high noon when he rode into the single street, eyes alert, straying from side to side. Although he imagined himself to be unknown here, there was always the possibility that Varges had spread the word around, together with his description and there might be men on the look out for him, hoping to pick up some reward money for his capture, dead or alive.

The street seemed oddly empty but with the full heat of the noonday sun glaring down from a hot, brassy heaven, it did not seem out of the ordinary. He tethered his mount in front of the saloon, and went inside to slake his thirst. It had been dusty riding along that trail and the back of his throat felt parched, clogged with the white dust kicked up by the hoofs of his horse. The saloon was almost empty and he walked straight up to the bar, the barkeep eyeing him suspiciously for a moment. There was no recognition in his eyes even though it had been the same man that had served him when he had been in Chandler City only a few days before. But, he guessed, there were plenty of men like him, saddle-tramps on the face of it, who rode into town, stayed for one day, two at the most, then rode on again and never came back. Bums who passed through and were gone, drifting along the narrow, winding trails, possibly one jump ahead of the law.

He drank a sharp thirst down, then turned to the bar keep. 'Reckon you could rustle me up a meal?' he asked.

The other gave him a quick glance, then jerked a thumb in the direction of the room leading off the main room.

'Through there,' he said harshly. 'I'll bring it to you in five minutes. Lucky for you that we're quiet at the moment. Bacon and eggs do for you?'

'They'll do fine.' Clint nodded. He walked through into the smaller room and seated himself at one of the plain wooden tables. The meal came a few minutes later, and the barkeep stood over him as he had that other time, looking down at him, eyes full of enquiry.

Clint ate a few mouthfuls, then glanced up. 'Mebbe you could help me,' he said quietly. 'I'm looking for someone.'

'Everybody who comes here is looking for somebody,' said the fat man. He shook his head and spread his hands out wide. 'Either it's the law or somebody looking for revenge. Mebbe that's why there ain't no law and order in Chandler City, why that rancher Donovan can ride in here and shoot the place to pieces whenever he feels like it.'

Clint made to say that he was working for Donovan, then thought better of it. Evidently this man was taking no sides, but when someone came riding in with a bunch of men determined to shoot up the place, it was inevitable that windows would be shattered and furniture smashed and that was all men such as this cared about. If he wanted to get information from the other, he had better keep his mouth shut about knowing Donovan, he decided.

'The person I'm looking for is a woman, about twenty-five or so, tall, dark hair, dark eyes. She dressed as if she comes from back east, but there's something about her that marks her out as a westerner. Know where I might find her? It's important.'

He held out a twenty dollar bill in his left hand so that the other could see it clearly. The man's eyes widened a shade and for a moment his mind seemed to be working around the question, as though deliberating within himself just why Clint should want to know the where-abouts of such a woman. Then he nodded his head, took the money and stuffed it into the voluminous pocket of his white apron. 'There can be only the one woman in town who answers to that description. You must be meaning Miss Ashton.'

'I'm afraid I don't know her name,' admitted Clint. He chewed on a mouthful of food, noticed the look of suspicion that flared into the barkeep's eyes, then went on hastily, 'She saved my life once, and I'd like to repay her. Is she still in Chandler City?'

The other shrugged. 'She was an hour ago. Saw her out on the street. She's put up at the hotel yonder. She doesn't seem to be the real friendly type. I doubt if you'll even get to see her.'

'Reckon I can but try.' Clint finished his meal, drank the hot coffee, then tossed a couple of coins on to the table and went out. The hotel was just on the other side of the street and he left his horse outside the saloon while he stepped across. Inside the lobby, he saw the desk clerk watching him carefully, as if a little unsure of him. Clint went up to the desk, dragging spurs across the thick carpet.

'I'm sorry.' The clerk shook his head. 'We're fully booked up. Every room is occupied.'

'I'm not looking for a room,' Clint told him, leaning forward over the desk. 'I'd like to speak to one of your guests here – Miss Ashton. I understand that she is staying here.'

'Why . . . yes.' The other swallowed nervously. 'But I'm not sure if she'll see anyone. She usually stays in her room. What name shall I give?'

'That won't be necessary.' Clint pushed himself upright. 'Just tell me the number of her room and I'll go up and surprise her.' He knew with certainty that if the clerk gave his name, it would mean nothing to her and even if it did, she might refuse to see him. For a moment the other hesitated, then his glance fell swiftly as Clint moved his hand down until his fingers closed over the butt of one of the guns at his waist. 'She's in Room Fourteen,' said the other, his voice pitched a little higher than normal. 'But we don't want any trouble here, this is a respectable place and—' But he was talking to thin air. Clint was already striding up the wide stairs, spurs jingling a little. He found Room Fourteen without difficulty and rapped loudly on the door.

For a moment, there was silence, then a woman's clear voice called: 'Yes, who is it?'

He did not reply, but knocked again and heard footsteps moving towards the door and a moment later, it opened and he found himself looking into the dark eyes which had haunted him so often since that day when he had seen her watching him as Donovan and his men had fought to extricate themselves from the trap which had been set for them in the street outside.

Recognition was immediate. For a moment she stood there, looking him up and down, then she said quickly 'What are you doing here? I never thought I'd see you again after the trouble you got yourself into in Dodge.'

'That's one of the things I want to talk to you about,' he said hurriedly, as she made to close the door. 'I've got to talk to you now that I've finally found you. I think that you owe me this anyway.'

She paused for a moment, then a faint smile touched her lips and she opened the door wider, stepping on one side to allow him to enter. He went inside, feeling suddenly awkward. There was an air of feminity about the place which made him feel uneasy. It had been so long since he had been in a place like that that he felt a little confused as he stood there, looking at her.

She kept her eyes on him, frank and open, and there was that strange interest in them that quickened his pulse as it had never been quickened before. He went forward a couple of paces, said hesitantly: 'You saw what happened in Dodge. I know that you witnessed everything. And you must have known that I was on trial there for my life. Varges brought in half a dozen men who perjured them-

146

selves, lied when they said that I'd shot them down in cold blood. Why didn't you come forward then to clear my name?'

She bit her lip and turned away from him suddenly, shoulders bowed a little. In a very small voice, she said: 'I couldn't do that. All I could hope for then was that you might be able to get away from that jail before they hung you.' For a moment, she stood like that, then turned just as abruptly to face him and there was something in her face and eyes that took him by surprise. 'Does it surprise you to know that when they were planning that lynching party, I was in Dodge too trying to find some way of getting you out of jail. I was with them, ready to shoot the first man to put a rope around your neck. But by that time you had broken out yourself.'

'Wouldn't it have been easier to stand up in that court-room and tell them all the truth? In the face of the evidence, I reckon that the sheriff's pack of lies would have crashed about him.'

'You don't understand and I'm afraid I can't tell you anything about that at the moment.' She came right up to him, took him by the arm. 'Can't you trust me for just a little longer, then I'll tell you everything you want to know.'

'I don't find it very easy to trust a woman who seemed to be perfectly willing to let an innocent man hang,' he retorted. He still felt uneasy, not sure how far he could trust her. There was just the chance that she was working with Varges and this could be another trap that he had walked into with his eyes shut. Then she smiled up at him and the smile went warm into him. The veiled expression in her eyes suddenly lifted for a moment and he saw want come into her. He put his hands on her shoulders, swayed her against him and kissed her full on the lips and she did not draw back as he had expected that she would. Rather she seemed to tighten her arms around his neck, then she released her hold and stepped back.

147

'I think I've been waiting for you to do that ever since I saw you that night in town – it seems like an age ago, but it can only be a few days.'

'I often wondered about you, even before Varges picked me up on a trumped up charge of murder.' He paused, thought of the other reason why he had headed into Chandler City. He gave the girl a studying glance, wondering if she might be able to help him. She seemed to know her way around this town – and Dodge too – and it would help if he could find out from a source he imagined he could trust.

'Do you know if Sheriff Varges came into Chandler City any time in the past few days, if he talked with any of the roughnecks, the gamblers and rustlers here?'

Her lips parted a little and she looked up at him in surprise. 'Why do you ask that?' she queried. 'And how do you know that he came here?'

Clint smiled tightly. 'So he has been here, trying to enlist the help of these men?'

'Well, yes. But that's no concern of yours. Or have you decided that you'll fight Varges anyway you can now that you're free?'

'I've got my own reasons for asking,' he told her, still keeping his hands on her shoulders. 'And it has to do with Varges in a way. He's been riding me for some time now. I want a chance to pay him back.'

She caught him urgently and her voice was tight as she said quickly, 'Don't get yourself mixed up in this. You don't know what is happening. Yes, Varges came here the day before yesterday, rounded up some of the rustlers and started giving them orders. He's going to do something which certainly has nothing to do with the law in Dodge, though I've suspected for some time that he's no real lawman. But there are a score of men ready to travel with him tonight. You don't stand a chance against a band like that. Keep out of it whatever you do and let your revenge

148

wait for a better moment if you have to go through with it at all.'

He shrugged. Whatever happened, he did not want her to know the real reason behind his questions. If any of those rustlers got to her, they would stop at nothing to make her talk if they thought she knew anything. 'All right, I won't go after them alone. I'll wait until I have men with me,' he said, choosing his words carefully so that he did not actually lie to her. 'But I won't be able to stay long in town. I'm riding out in a little while. When can I see you again?'

'Somehow, I don't think it will be very long.' She smiled as she spoke and he had the impression that she was holding out on him. 'But be more careful with yourself than you have been in the past.'

'I'll try,' he promised. She watched him for a moment, her face shadowed and soft. Then she moved over to the door. 'You'd better go now before that clerk downstairs gets suspicious and starts asking questions.'

When Clint rode back along the trail to the Donovan ranch, he knew most of what was happening in Chandler City. As Varges had claimed, there were at least twenty gunmen ready to ride out shortly after dark in support of Carswell and the outlaws from the hills.

At the ranch, he found most of the men already saddled up, some carrying rifles. Donovan came out a moment later, stood in the porch, a high-powered rifle in his right hand. Clint rode up to the ranch-house, slid from the saddle and walked over to him.

Donovan grinned, his black beard jutting out aggressively. 'You find out anything in Chandler City, Clint?'

'Plenty.' The other nodded. 'Seems like Varges was telling the truth about those rustlers riding out to join up with Carswell. There must be twenty of 'em at least. They can't be far behind me on the trail.'

'We're all set to ride,' said Donovan evenly. 'This time we

mean business. We're going to wipe out this threat once and for all. This is the chance we've waited for, to get them both together.'

'It isn't going to be easy,' muttered Clint dubiously. Now that he had seen something of the men waiting in Chandler City, he felt a little unsure of himself. He did not doubt that he would be able to play his part in the gunfight which was looming up, but he was unsure about the rest of the men. They had little stake in this and yet they were being asked to risk their lives. And there was also the inescapable point that they would be outnumbered by at least two-to-one.

'Have you figured how we're going to get word through to that first stage to bring the men back when we need 'em?' he asked tightly.

The other nooded slowly. 'We've asked Varges a few more questions since you left, Clint. He talked a lot more. Seems there'll be about ten minutes between the two stages. I'll have a couple of my men posted further along the trail with orders to stop that first stage. It won't be easy, I know, because the men in it will be looking for trouble and it's going to take a lot of quick talk to convince them in time that my men aren't members of the Carswell gang, setting them up for an ambush. They'll be trigger happy in that stage, ready to shoot at anything that moves.'

'That's a chance we've got to take,' muttered Clint quietly He turned his glance to the men who sat easily in their saddles waiting for the order to move out. 'They all know what they have to do?'

'Yes, every one of them. I know that I can trust them to do as they've been told. They realize the importance of this just as much as we do.'

'But it's their lives that we're dicing with,' Clint told him evenly, keeping all feeling out of his voice.

Donovan made a gesture with his hand, a movement too of his broad shoulders. 'We're used to trouble like this in this territory. Whenever we ride into Chandler City we can expect to be shot at from cover by the men there. Now is the time to put an end to all that. This is perhaps the only time when we'll get those two sides together, in the same place, and at our advantage. They won't be expecting any trouble from us. All they'll be looking for will be the men in the stage. And they'll be prepared for that. You can be sure that Chet Carswell will have laid his plans well now that Varges has told him everything.'

The negro servant came out with a mug of hot coffee, handed it to Clint. He drank it gratefully, feeling it wash some of the dust out of his mouth. Then he tightened the belt around his waist, checked his guns, eased them once or twice in their holsters, then mounted up. Donovan brought his horse up beside him. 'Reckon you know this spot where they plan to ambush the stage better than I do,' he said. 'You seemed to have plenty of success there last night. We'll follow if you'll lead the way.'

Clint's answer was quick nod of the head. He touched spurs to the horse's flanks and moved out from the ranch. Sitting tall and straight in the saddle, all of the weariness of the day forgotten in the knowledge that the time had now come for the showdown, he squinted up at the moon lying low on the eastern horizon. There would again be plenty of light by which to see, he decided. So long as they reached that spot before Carswell and his killers, they stood a good chance of defeating them, of whipping them for good.

They passed over the long meadow which blended almost imperceptibly into the wider stretch of the rangeland. Only two men watched the herd now. The rest were riding with them. There would be no trouble from the rustlers on that particular night with every man riding for Carswell. For once, perhaps the only night, the herd would be safe.

Beyond the boundary fence, the trail ran in a series of

twisting dog-legs towards the mountains which bulked up on their ride as they struck off in a tight bunch in the direction of Dodge. Clint sat tall and straight in the saddle, his eyes moving all the time, his keen gaze quartering the horizon on all sides, alert for the first sign of the rustlers. He doubted if they would run into the men from the hills on this part of the trail. They would cut down from the 'Lost Horizon' mine workings by that narrow, twisting trail which he and the others had taken the previous night.

But the rough country to their left stretched away clear to the river which separated it from the desert, and all of it was empty, devoid of any movement. In the moonlight, it seemed to shimmer eerily, with a pale glow that played tricks with his eyes, making him see flickering shadows that were not really there. But he followed them just the same, making certain that it was not a bunch of horsemen in the distance, cutting over the rocks and sand in their direction.

In between watching for the men from Chandler City, Clint eyed the men who rode with him with a growing alertness. He let his lips loosen and pulled in a deep breath of the cool, winey air which flowed down in a soft pressure against his face from the slopes of the mountains. The men rode wrapped in silence. Even Donovan seemed wrapped up in his own thoughts and it was difficult to guess from that inscrutable face what he was thinking. Time and again, Clint thought back to Ruth Ashton. There was still that air of mystery about her, even though he had seen her, knew her name and a little about her. What was a girl like that doing in Chandler City anyway? he wondered. She belonged back east where women wore that kind of finery, not here in this rough, new country. This was the place for the homesteaders, the pioneers. Not for women like her. And yet he had a vague idea that there was more to her than that. There had seemed to be a purpose about the way she looked and moved.

He tried to visualise her face in his mind's eye, for he needed something tangible like that to hold on to, knowing what they were riding into. Chet Carswell was throwing in everything into this gamble. If it paid off, he would be the richest man in the state if not in the whole of the west. Why in God's name had the company decided to send all that gold by stage? he asked himself fiercely. Why could they not have taken it by rail as they had in the past. There were ways of protecting it then which were not available to them here on the trail. Five men in the stage which carried the bullion, and the best part of their force several minute's drive ahead, out of reach unless those two men that Donovan had instructed to fetch the coach back succeeded in their task and in time.

He felt more and more unsettled as they rode along the trail, heading for the spot where, if Varges could be believed on that important point, the ambush was to take place. If there was any doubt in Donovan's mind, none of it showed through on to his face. He sat in the saddle, broadshouldered, staring straight ahead into the moonlight. A dark-visaged man fighting his own private war against these men. To him, this was probably just like a military campaign in which everything could be foreseen and all probabilities envisaged and worked out in advance. But it wouldn't be like that at all. They were facing Chet Carswell now, a man who knew nothing of military strategy; a man who gave orders only to kill, who lived by the sixgun and who knew only that kind of law.

Forty minutes and they came within sight of the tall walls of rock which hemmed in the track at that point. Clint slowed his mount, lifted his hand to stop the others.

'There's the place,' he said tightly, pointing. 'If they aren't here yet, then it won't be long before they arrive. That stage will be passing this point in less than an hour from now.'

'Then we'll get the men into position.' Donovan cast

about him, his dark eyes seaching the area, picking out the most likely spot where the horses could be safely hidden out of sight of probing eyes and the men could command the best area of fire once the rustlers and outlaws moved in on the trail.

Clint got down from the saddle, eyes drifting back toward the trail behind them. Not long now before the men from Chandler City arrived and by that time, every man had to be hidden.

Clint turned slightly on the hard ground. Lifting his head a little, he could just make out the bunch of horsemen less than fifty yards away. The men from Chandler City had arrived, were still in the saddle, waiting at the southern end of the gap in the rocks through which the trail passed. Beyond them, in the rocks where the trail from the hills met the main stage trail into Dodge, he could just make out the other men who had come riding down that trail a few moments earlier Even from that distance, the moonlight was bright enough for him to make out the tall, burly figure of Chet Carswell, seated astride his huge black stallion which it was claimed no other man could handle. The sight of the man stirred the old hatred within him and his fingers tightened convulsively around the butt of the Colts. For a moment, he remembered how they had said this man had laughed when he had killed his parents. Possibly the other had even forgotten the incident, for there had been others since that day. He brought his mind back to the present. Beside him, Donovan shifted closer to him, keeping his head well down. His mouth was tight as he whispered, 'That first stage should be due through here any minute.'

'There's something now,' Clint murmured. 'I can just hear it along the trail. Coming up fast by the sound of it.'

Less than three minutes later, the stage came thundering along the trail, entered the shadow between the rising walls of rock. Clint could hear the thunder of the horses hoofs reflected back and muffled by the rock and even though he knew that it would be allowed to go through unmolested, his mind kept listening for a sudden shot But a few moments later, the stage came out into the open again, curved away around the bend and was gone in a cloud of kicked-up dust.

The tension which had mounted swiftly at the sudden sound, began to fade a little, only to rise again as each man realized that in less than ten minutes time, the stage carrying a fortune in gold bars and dust would be following the first and that was when the trouble would start.

The minutes seemed to stretch themselves out into individual eternities as they waited for the second stage. A break in their favour, thought Clint tensely, had delivered Varges into their hands and he had talked. A second break in the same direction was needed now. He had cast his eyes over the men with Carswell and knew that they would have a stiff fight on their hands against these combined bands.

When the sound of the oncoming stage reached his ears, it seemed as if he had been hearing it for a long time and it had only just registered on his tired mind. He forced himself to listen intently, then knew that he was not mistaken. He eased himself into a fresh position, saw the men near him tense automatically. Every single muscle in his body was so tight that he began to ache and the muscles of his legs were cramped painfully. He chewed hard on his lower lip, turning his head slightly in an attempt to pick out the stage before it reached the rocks.

Finally, he saw it, a lumbering shape in the moonlight. Those men inside it must be wondering whether their ruse had succeeded, he thought tightly, or whether the information had leaked and Carswell knew everything.

The first shot, ringing along the narrow walls of the canyon, seemed to hit his eardrums with the physical shock

155

of a hammer blow. More shots followed and a moment later, the coach rumbled out into the open, then swung to a halt as a crowd of men rode their horses directly in front of it, shying the animals in the harness. The man on top of the coach, alongside the driver, tried to bring his rifle to bear on the men riding down out of the hills, but before he could loose off a single shot against the attackers, he threw up his arms and dropped sideways off the coach.

Swiftly, filled suddenly with a savage exultation, Clint rose to feet and ran forward, the guns blazing in his hands. Two of the outlaws fell before the men knew the direction from which the fire was coming. Several others wheeled their mounts, turning swiftly, in an attempt to ride them down. Clint went down on one knee, fired up at two men who tried to converge on him as he knelt among the rocks. The first man fell forward, over his horse's neck and crashed into the rocks less than two feet from where Clint knelt, firing instinctively at the second man. He felt a slug burn its way along his arm and almost lost his   hold on the gun as pain lanced redly into his shoulder   muscles.

Beside him, Donovan let out a bull-like roar of defiance and loosed off a couple of shots that hammered into the man, knocking him backward in the saddle, so that his legs went up into the air and with a loud, wild cry he fell back, one leg suddenly caught in the reins, so that the horse, stampeding at the sudden noise, dragged his body across the rocks as it turned and galloped off into the distance.

Scrambling to his feet, Clint worked his way towards the coach, now standing in the middle of the trail. There were still men milling around it and he could pick out Carswell's voice, booming orders above the rest. The men inside the coach were firing now into the milling crowd. Two of the outlaws threw up their arms and fell, guns dropping from their nerveless fingers. But they still outnumbered Donovan's men and slowly they began to force them back into the rocks.

Reluctantly, Clint ducked into the rocks, throwing his body flat as lead hummed viciously over his shoulders, spitting against the hard rock behind him, whining into the darkness in murderous ricochet. Donovan was somewhere in the moonlight, rallying the men as they began to fall back. Clint gritted his teeth. Whatever happened, they had to keep those men away from that stage. Once Carswell had his hands on the gold, he could ride off into the hills and lose them before they could catch him.

Deliberately exposing himself, he ran forward, dodging from one patch of shadow to another. Most of the outlaws had ridden away from the trail in their efforts to run down Donovan and his men and a few were watching the stage. A few moments later, he reached the smooth side of the rocks which loomed high over the trail and began to scramble up them. His arm began to ache intolerably and every movement he made seemed to make it worse, but he gritted his teeth and kept on moving until he reached the boulders which littered the top of the rocky wall. Directly below him lay the stage, the horses still milling around aimlessly in the traces. For a moment, he paused, balancing the guns in his hands. Then he saw the two men moving in from both sides. One he recognized instantly as Chet Carswell. Bracing himself, he jumped, hit the nearer man on the shoulders, taking him to the ground. A bullet from inside the coach zipped past his head as he reversed one of his own guns and struck the man viciously behind the ear with the butt. He collapsed without a sound on to the hard earth.

Sucking air into his heaving lungs, Clint rose to his feet, ran forward. Behind him, the firing had burst out anew and he felt a sudden surge of hope as he realized that Donovan and his men were still fighting.

Swiftly, he ran around the back of the coach, then halted in his tracks. Chet Carswell faced him in the moonlight with a sneer on his face, the gun in his hand pointed directly Clint's chest.

'So you're the *hombre* who's been hounding me,' he grunted. 'Reckon you and I have a score to settle. Once I've done that I'm going to take this gold and get out of this territory. But you're going to die first just as Bart and Brad died.'

Clint saw his knuckle whiten as he increased the pressure on the trigger and subconsciously, he braced himself for the leaden impact of the bullet as it smashed through his body. He knew inwardly that he could never bring his own guns up in time to stop him.

The shot sounded a second later and involuntarily, Clint winced, several seconds passing before he realized that Carswell had not fired, that he still held his gun in his hand, although it was already beginning to slip from his fingers as the look of hate on his face smoothed itself out into one of blank amazement. Then he pitched forward, arms and legs jerking grotesquely before he finally hit the ground. Instinctively, Clint turned towards the stage, found himself looking into dark eyes which watched him with concern.

'Ruth!' Somehow, he got the word out. 'What in God's name are you doing here?'

'No time to answer that now,' she said swiftly. There was a note of assured competence in her voice that surprised him. 'He's dead, but the others are still alive and dangerous. How are your men faring?'

'We can't hold them much longer,' he said harshly. 'There are too many of them. The other Carswell brothers are still alive and they'll continue to fight so long as there's any chance at all of getting their hands on the gold.'

She nodded quickly as another burst of firing came from the side of the trail. Clint moved swiftly to the other side of the stage. Two men swung out of the shadows, rode straight at him, firing as they came. Swiftly, he threw himself down as they raced past. Bullets hammered into the woodwork of the coach and he knew instinctively, that unless a miracle happened they were finished. He tried to lift his head, to see whether Donovan and many of the others were still alive, aware of the faint drumming in his head, the throbbing at the back of his temples. Then, in one wild moment of understanding, he knew what that throbbing, drumming sound was and he turned his head with a sudden jerk and stared back along the trail. Even as the outlaws tried to turn and run, he saw the other stage grind to a halt. Gunfire poured into the fleeing men as they tried to escape into the hills. Most of them were cut down before they could get under cover. Now they wanted only one thing, to escape. All thought of the gold had been forgotten They realized now that the odds against them were heavy and their chances of escape slim.

Clint pushed his guns back into their holsters. He could safely leave any pursuit of the outlaws to Donovan and the men in the first stage. He went back to the other coach and opened the door. Ruth Ashton climbed down, stood for a moment looking up at him. Then a faint smile spread over her face.

'It's finished,' she said softly. 'We've broken them for good. With Chet dead and his brothers either dead or wounded, we need never fear them again.'

'You promised that when it was over you'd explain why—' he began, but she stopped him.

'Why I didn't testify in your defence back in Dodge,' she said solemnly. There was a strange look on her face. 'I couldn't. You see, I'm a Pinkerton agent. My job was to make sure that we captured or killed Chet Carswell when he tried for the gold. Whatever happened, I didn't want anybody in Dodge to know that the men you had killed were two of the Carswell brothers. Besides, when you were in jail,

I thought there might just be the chance that the Carswells would ride into Dodge to get you out of jail. If they had, we would have been ready for them. As it was, they didn't, and once you escaped I knew that things were bound to come to a showdown.'

He thought about that for a moment then said: 'I guess they'll have to find some other agent to do their work for them from now on. This country is good. I want to stay here, make my roots here and I want you with me.' The way he said it struck her powerfully and the pressure of her hands on his answered his unspoken question for him.